A WINTER'S WEDDING

CHRISTMAS COVE
BOOK THREE

SARAH DRESSLER

5 PRINCE PUBLISHING
5PRINCEBOOKS.COM

Published by 5 PRINCE PUBLISHING & BOOKS, LLC

PO Box 865, Arvada, CO 80001

www.5PrinceBooks.com

ISBN digital: 978-1-63112-384-9

ISBN print: 978-1-63112-385-6

Cover Credit: Marianne Nowicki

F103124

To all the couples out there waiting for the right time.

ACKNOWLEDGMENTS

Thank you to my husband and children for your steadfast belief in me, and for our own road-trip to Las Vegas over a decade ago that inspired much of this tale.

Thank you to the 5 Prince team for your continued guidance and encouragement.

Thank you to my editor, Cate, for helping my stories come to life.

Thank you to my early readers, Racheal and Jennifer, for your critical feedback.

Finally, thanks to all my loyal readers for loving my novels. Your enthusiasm feeds my desire to tell more stories.

ALSO BY SARAH DRESSLER

A WINTER'S WEDDING

CHAPTER 1

There were plenty of times when Leo could have surprised his fiancée with a grand romantic gesture, though he questioned whether showing up in Las Vegas while she was on a writing assignment was the best time to do it. Trusting his friend's suggestion, Leo hopped on a flight and prayed for the best. Even though the wedding was a week away, he probably should have known better than to add anything stressful to America's already full planner, but with what he had arranged, she would have no choice but to forgive his impulsive expression of love—or so he hoped.

He raised an arm to the amber sky in the south, Leo hailed a ride-share outside the airport's sliding doors and readjusted his wireless earbud. "I'm just glad I made it here in one piece. The turbulence was bad coming down into the valley. Remind me to never get on a plane again."

"You're flying to Italy next week," Cam said in his ear.

A disgruntled sigh vibrated in Leo's throat. "That's next week's problem. Does she suspect anything?" Leo said and ducked inside the car that had pulled up to the curb.

"She's been texting with Jenny all morning. She's at the dress shop," Cam said. "Take a deep breath, bro. Everything is set. The hotel, dinner, everything."

Cam, Leo's best friend since moving to the Cove years ago, and the only other person his own age at the time, was one of those guys that just knew how to get things done. He was always calm, and he was always ready to have a good time. Ever since Cam had become a father a year ago, he had been living vicariously through the other young couples in town. In this instance, he had thought up and planned the whole Valentine's surprise in Vegas. "Thanks, man."

"Where to?" the driver asked.

"The city of love," Leo sighed.

The driver cleared his throat as though he was annoyed at the vague answer.

"Paris. Take me to the Paris Hotel, please."

"You've got it bad. I don't know what she sees in you," Cam laughed, "but you're lucky to have her."

Leo was acutely aware of just how lucky he was to have found America, and how blessed he was by her determination and hopeful spirit. "I don't know why I'm so nervous about this."

"Because you've never done anything like this before?"

"I appreciate you talking me down. I'm planning on surprising her right after her interviews for the magazine."

"Whatever you do, have a good time."

"Will do, boss."

The line went dead just as the car turned north up the storied Las Vegas Strip and joined the steady flow of light traffic. Las Vegas Boulevard was practically empty during the midday hours except for the section of road that butted up against the iconic 'Welcome to Fabulous Las Vegas' sign. He'd seen the location countless times featured in movies and television shows, but the attraction looked considerably larger in person than he thought it would.

Up ahead, the striking silhouette of the pyramid at the Luxor

Casino peeked out from behind the golden towers of the Mandalay Bay resort. Stopping at the intersection with the New York New York hotel on the left and the emerald façade of the MGM hotel to his right, he shook his head that he was actually there.

"How long you in town for?" the driver asked in an attempt to break the silence that filled the vehicle.

"Only a night. I'm surprising my fiancée for Valentine's Day."

"Are you in town for the Guinness record try?"

"Sort of, actually. But we're not getting married here. She's a writer for a magazine and is covering the event. We're getting married back home next week."

America was working on the human-interest portion of the city that sees more weddings each year than any other city in the world, and tomorrow, there was a plan to break the world record for the most marriages in one place at one time. America almost didn't take the assignment since it was so close to her own wedding day, and there were so many last-minute details to take care of, but Leo knew there was no person better at Jet Trek Magazine to take on the story than his beautiful bride-to-be. So, when her wedding dress designer agreed to send the gown to Las Vegas for the final fitting, saving her an extra trip back to the store in New York, taking the assignment was that much more appealing.

Things just work out for the best sometimes, which is why Leo had decided to jump on a plane and head westward as well. In a year that had thrown more challenges at him than he could count, he had learned that the hard things can become easy, and the easy things can become beautiful. Leo also knew Murphy's laws well enough to know how to count his blessings whenever he first noticed them.

The traffic light turned green, and Leo spotted the fountains of Bellagio spraying high into the sky. A breeze scattered the water droplets and looked like misty snowflakes floating back to the ground. The steel struts of the Eiffel Tower came into view across from the fountains. Its light-gray structure shined in the noontime light, with thousands of glass bulbs capturing the sunrays.

Placing a hand over his thumping heart, Leo felt a smile pull at his cheeks at the rising anticipation. The car slowed and turned right past a brightly painted blue and gold hot air balloon. The driveway circled a replica of the Arc de Triomphe, which so happened to be being used as a billboard for some comedy act that he'd never heard of before. A sleek black limousine came alongside Leo to his right and parked under a green glass overhang, while his car pulled into a fully exposed and less important drop-off area.

"Here we are," the driver said. "That'll be twenty dollars and seventy-seven cents."

Leo opened his black leather wallet and thumbed through the edges of the bills tucked neatly inside. He handed a twenty and a five up to the cabby's waiting grip. "Keep the change."

"Have a nice stay, mister."

Leo stepped from the car, with only his small overnight bag over his shoulder. "Highway robbery," he said and patted the roof of the small sedan, indicating he could go. From where he stood, the top half or so of the replica Eiffel Tower peeked above the surrounding rooflines, designed to mimic a Parisian street, and gleamed in the daylight. The creation was magnificently imposing, and he wondered just how big the real one in France was compared to this one. *Far over my head,* he thought. "Just like me being here."

CHAPTER 2

America sat alone in the luxurious fitting room, though it felt more like a pressure cooker threatening to overheat her nerves. She had become so accustomed to not checking her watch every other minute like she used to do before Leo showed her that life can be a little slower sometimes, that now—as she checked the time for a third instance in sixty seconds—she knew she needed a break from all of the wedding planning stress. How arranging something so wonderful could feel so dreadful, she would dig into later. Much later. For now, America just needed to tick off the last few items on her to do list, one at a time.

With a week to go to her big day, her reception menu still needed finalizing, her flowers were waiting to be handpicked, and her maid of honor had a final dress fitting scheduled. All the while, she was on assignment halfway across the country. With each passing month of planning, and the more hands that stirred the pot, she became increasingly nervous, wanting everything to go off perfectly.

The whole town of Christmas Cove was expecting her wedding to Leopold Thorpe, the former mayor, to be a grand bash. Last year, when she bought the old pink Victorian mansion, the town had accepted her into the fold just like family. She had received such a beautiful welcome that she knew there was no other town for her. While renovating her home, many people had chipped in with their power tool prowess or lent an extra hand with the demo. Her house had become a beacon of hope for the beleaguered town, and the wedding was a way she could thank everyone.

The wedding was to be the centerpiece for a place that was still healing from years of neglect and depression. *No pressure*, she thought. America was about to check her watch again when she heard the delicate clacking of stilettos on the polished wood floor outside the fitting room door. Her breath caught with each pound of her heart against her lungs.

This was it. The moment she had been waiting eight months for. Dress fitting day.

"Knock, knock," the stylist's voice sang out from the other side of the door.

America looked around the quiet, creamy space as she stood from the gold velvet chair and caught her reflection in the oversized mirror leaning against one wall. Her skin was radiant against her white silk robe. Her chocolate hair lay in long waves down her back, the way she planned to wear it on the big day, and her cheeks were rosy, but natural. She smiled and the water works began cranking behind her eyes.

"Come in," America said.

"I've got it right here," the cheery woman said. "Are you ready to see it?"

Of course she was ready. Does any bride, standing nearly naked in a bridal fitting room, not want to see what they've paid for? Her excitement was tainted with the fear that after months of waiting, her dress wouldn't be right. She was unable to speak as she concentrated on keeping her emotions in check. She took another controlled breath and nodded to the woman. As the woman took hold of the zipper and unveiled the dress with torturous drama, America's heartbeat seemed to vibrate with the same speed as the ticking of the tiny zipper fingers snapping apart.

Reaching the top, the stylist slipped the white satin garment bag over the hanger arms and fluffed the dress's layers out from the bottom of the bag.

Cream and white tulle spilled out onto the floor in the middle of the room. The dress was big. Bigger than America remembered, but she would withhold judgment until it was on her body. So many things can happen in eight months, which is a short time to wait for a wedding dress to be produced, that she wondered how any bride was completely happy with their choice by the time of the actual wedding day, especially if that wait time was significantly more that hers had been.

As it was, she and Leo had already waited over a year to get married. They had only known each other for a couple of weeks when they got engaged on Christmas Day. A long engagement had been prudent, and it allowed them to really get to know one another. Early on, they had faced many challenges. Their courtship began during a time when Leo's beloved town, Christmas Cove, was incorporated into the limits of a neighboring city. A few months later, a late spring storm had nearly washed away The Foundry, Leo's freshly-opened retreat resort. Picking the day was the easiest part of the planning process; getting to the big day had been an exercise in fortitude.

America stepped into the dress opening and the stylist pulled the frock up her body. The skirt was big, like a snowball, but weighed nearly nothing. The dozens of tulle layers draped easily over her hips and cascaded to the floor like a fairytale princess gown. With a sweep of her arm over her shoulder, she moved her long dark waves around her neck and over the front of her shoulder. Holding the beaded bodice against her chest, the stylist threaded the corset strings back and forth for what seemed like an hour, though she didn't check her watch to confirm. The whole time, unable to see herself, as the mirrored wall was behind her, she looked down and inspected each perfectly-placed bead and fluffy layer.

The craftmanship was incredible and took her breath away. Or maybe it was the laces being tightened up her back and restricting her lungs, but the effect was the same, tears. The water began to drip before she was fully laced in. As the stylist stashed the bow strings into a flap at her lower back and picked up the back of the dress, America knew she was in for a smeared-mascara kind of morning.

"I'll follow you out?" the consultant said. America tried to turn towards the mirror but was rebuked by a single finger pressing into her spine. "Out. You should see it out there. Trust me."

America did as she was instructed and walked out into the main salon. Round, cream-colored velvet sofas faced a central three-sided mirror, each with a pedestal positioned directly in front. Two stunning brides occupied their respective places around the central mirror, and an audible gasp escaped from one of them as America approached. America's mind whirled. *Is it that bad*, she panicked?

"Now watch your step," the stylist said as they turned towards the mirror.

America's eyes were trained downward to where her feet usually were though she could only see the semi-sheer mohair mesh trim along the bottom edges of the tulle layers. She lifted the front of the skirt and perched herself in the center of the round pedestal.

"Gorgeous," one of the other bride's guests whispered.

"Like a princess. I wonder who she is?" another whispered and caused America to chuckle into her throat.

She was a no-one, in reality. Unless someone regularly consumed online travel magazine articles, there was little chance that her modest celebrity had escaped into the wider world of would-be bridal parties.

America had not yet looked in the mirror's reflection. Standing behind her, the stylist parachuted the train of the gown with a large swing of her arms. As the billow settled and the tulle came to rest on the floor, the woman said, "You can look now, America."

Though hesitating wasn't something she was accustomed to doing, she lifted her wrist just enough to glimpse the time. She had to hurry up, or she would risk being late for her next meeting. She pushed a breath through pursed lips, dabbed the dampness from under her eyes with the back of her forefinger, and lifted her gaze.

The skirt glittered in the light emanating from crystal LED's rimming the mirror in front of her and from the chandelier hanging overhead. Sheets of fine netting terminated at her natural waist, though the oversized proportion of the skirt compared to the cinched tightness of the bodice caused her waist to appear dramatically thin.

Her fingers floated above the swirls of beads that wrapped around her curves and gave the impression of little hearts. The cherished shape was fitting for a wedding during the month of love, February, and she had known this dress was *the dress* at the first sight of the pretty symbology.

"Well? Is it everything you dreamed?"

America nodded and sniffled the meldrop from the tip of her nose. "It's perfect. Everyone will love it."

The stylist stepped away and America was helpless to set her eyes on anything else in the salon. She was a vision in white as bright as winter snow. Until that moment, the gravity of the situation had failed to fully hit. Sure, she had managed everyone's expectations well —even her own— but she was about to marry her best friend. The man that had so wonderfully helped her out of her own way and showed her a different kind of life. Leo had swept her away with his charm and gentle heart. Like the comfort of a cinnamon roll on a cold morning, he was everything she wanted in a partner and couldn't imagine a future without.

America Thorpe flashed in Broadway-style bulbs in her mind, though having a new last name would take some getting used to, she thought it had a nice ring to it. Leo Greene, on the other hand, sounded like the name of a lead guitarist of a wicked garage band. She held in a smirk as her mind settled back on taking Leo's name soon.

Pressing the tulle down in hopes the layers would settle a little more before next Saturday, there was no doubt that she would make a grand entrance walking down the aisle in front of the whole town looking the way she looked or smiling the way she was smiling. The blond man of her dreams would marry her, no matter how poofy her skirt was.

The stylist returned with an armful of white lace. "I brought a veil for you try on and—"

"Oh, I have one!" America exclaimed. "It's back in the fitting room." Taking one very wrong step off the pedestal, America stumbled over the front of her skirt and face-planted into the hard floor. She was pretty sure she wasn't dead as she lay staring at the glossy wood planks, though she wished she could rewind the last fifteen seconds of her life and have a redo.

"Goodness," the stylist said and came to America's aid. The whole tumble lasted mere seconds, but the embarrassment and concern was palpable in the eyes of the other brides there.

"Oh my gosh. I'm so mortified," America said, knowing the best way to defuse a moment was to name it for what it was. She straightened the dress and fluffed the skirt, but as she did, tiny crystals and seed beads spilled onto the ground like sugary sprinkles. What had been a straightforward embarrassment, was now a humiliation. Fear gripped America's gut at the fact that she might have just ruined her one and only wedding gown. "I am so sorry."

"It's not the end of the world," the woman said. "We can fix this, no problem. You'd be surprised how many beads need touching up after the final fitting. Happens all the time."

"Are you certain it's no trouble? I feel terrible," America said.

"I'm just glad you're alright. You stay here, I'll get the veil."

America returned to her position at the mirror while the stylist retrieved the lace and netting veil that had been a gift from her mother, Vivian. America squatted down low enough for the stylist to affix the comb into the hair at the crown of her head. When she stood tall, the veil topped off the white look and was the icing on the cake. She couldn't wait to see Leo's face at the wedding. She was a traditionalist and didn't want a first-look moment as was the trend amongst other brides. Rather, she wished to knock his socks off and witness his squirming and holding back tears along with all the other guests attending the ceremony.

"It's picture-perfect," America said.

"Congratulations," one of the other brides said as she stepped down from her own pedestal and headed back to a fitting room.

"Now, America, how long will you be in town? A note on your file says the wedding is in somewhere called Christmas Cove. So, I'm guessing you'll need a quick turnaround?" The stylist took America's hand and helped her down from the platform.

"I fly out tomorrow afternoon. Is that enough time?"

"I'll put a rush on the beading, and you're lucky this dress fits you like a glove and that you don't need additional alterations." Once safely back inside the fitting room, the stylist helped America out of the dress and rehung it inside the silk garment bag. "I'll take this to alterations right now and get you a firm time when you can come pick it up before you leave."

America slipped on her favorite jeans and checked the time. "I appreciate it. And again, I'm so sorry," America apologized as the woman set off and closed the door. After tugging on her white cable-knit sweater, she twisted her long hair into a fresh knot at the top of her head. Though it would have been nice for her mother to be at the fitting, she was glad no one she knew had been present there to witness her clumsiness. With her parents on a cruise for another couple of days, and the rest of her friends back home on the east coast, Las Vegas had seemed too big a place to go solo. But now, she could see there was a silver lining to having gone alone to her appointment.

America gathered her things and exited the fitting room. She had a little over an hour to get back to the hotel, change into her work clothing, and make it to the conference hall for her meeting. Out in the salon, she waited for word about the beading fix. One of the other brides was bouncing up and down, and nearly spilling out from the ill-fitting bodice between hugging her guests and crying. America couldn't help but grin at the joyful bride.

"Ms. Greene, thank you for waiting. Alterations say the earliest they can have it done is noon. Will that work with your travel plans?"

America's flight was scheduled for 4:17 the next afternoon. As the Las Vegas airport was small, she knew noon would allow her plenty of time to make her flight. "That will absolutely work. Thank you, again." She shook the woman's hand politely.

CHAPTER 3

America hurried through the wide corridor and entered the expansive ballroom at the Paris Hotel. Her heels made nearly no sound on the richly colored crimson and Parisian-blue carpet while she made her way to the center of the football field-sized space. *Christmas Cove could practically fit in here,* she thought as she approached the waiting hotel manager.

"You must be Ms. Greene. I'm Margarete, the crazy woman putting on this event." Margarete, who didn't look much older than America, who was in her late twenties, extended a hand in greeting.

Looking at the statuesque manager in her barbie-pink pencil skirt and light pink tight-fitting sweater, America wished she had chosen a flashier outfit for the occasion. Her black pixie trousers and crisp white button down didn't exactly scream wedding or Valentine's Day. At least she had thrown her sparkly silver stilettos onto her feet instead of the black ballet flats that she had originally plucked from her suitcase.

"I love your shoes," Margarete said unprompted and unknowingly affirmed America's last-minute decision.

"I love your whole..." America pointed with open palms up

and down in front of Margarete. "You look amazing, and so festive."

"There aren't many occasions to wear all pink, but the season of love is in the air. And this ballroom will look nothing like this tomorrow morning after our visual teams have their way with the space; pinks and reds splashed everywhere."

"I can't wait to see it all decked out. The ambiance will add an additional layer to my article for sure," America said and looked all around the space. Oversized white wall paneling was adorned with ornately carved mouldings that shined like mercury, while gold painted trim cased each section along the exterior walls. Overhead, more panels, and crystal chandeliers added to the room's grandeur. "If I didn't know better, I'd believe I was in France and not Nevada."

Margarete chuckled. "You won't find anything like this in France. Take it from a woman who grew up outside the real Paris in Montrouge. Las Vegas does French better than the French do. But don't tell anyone I said so," she whispered the last part.

This was a woman after America's own heart. Someone who wasn't afraid to see the world through her own lens. It was only too bad that Margarete wasn't planning to marry anyone at tomorrow's ceremony. America was certain that the Parisian woman would be an interesting interview subject.

"Now, I've got you set up right over here." Margarete gestured to a light blue Louis XIV style loveseat and coordinating chair. A small glass coffee table that featured antique gold legs separated the seating arrangement. "If you're ready, I'll send in the first couple."

Margarete turned and walked out the main double doors while America took a seat in the lone chair. Reaching into her sleek black tote, she retrieved a notebook and a small voice recorder that Poppy, her assistant turned best friend, had sent her a few months back for use in situations just like this one. Not that any of her other writing assignments had been anything *like this one* other than the traveling part.

In the year since being promoted to senior special interest writer, she had done no less than four featured articles. Her confidence had grown with each new published issue, along with her ability to let the heart of the story shine through. Even though she wrote for Jet Trek Magazine, she found a creative way to interweave the personal stories with the geographic locations. Jet Trek was a travel magazine, after all.

The first couple walked in with their hands tightly linked together in the narrow space between their bodies and made their way to the center of the huge room. Their eyes darted around the large space just as America had done upon entering the ballroom for the first time.

Knowing the pair may be nervous, she closed the distance and greeted them. "Come on over and have a seat," she said to the young couple. "My name is America, and I just want to thank you for agreeing to this interview today."

The man, boy rather, looked to be no more than nineteen years of age. His fiancée didn't appear to be any older, but the young woman was stunning. Shoulder-length brunette hair, cut into pretty layers, framed the girl's soft jawline. She wore a long baby-pink dress with ruffles across the bustline and tiny braided straps held everything up, which only accentuated her youthful features. The man wore a standard navy-blue suit. No tie, but a floral pocket square. Though young, they looked wonderful together.

"Firstly, congratulations." America took the recorder and held it out towards the couple. "I'll be recording this interview. Can you please state your full names and a verbal agreement to be recorded?"

"Darren Carpenter. I agree to be recorded." His accent was southern, the pretty kind that one hears in old movies.

"Brittney-Lynn Mayberry. I agree," she said in the same sweet way as Darren had spoken.

"Great. Let's start with the obvious. Are you excited to be getting married tomorrow?"

Brittney-Lynn's face lit up with a bright smile. "I've waited my whole life for this day."

America found that hard to believe since Brittney-Lynn still looked like a teenager. "And how many years is that?"

"Well," Brittney-Lynn began and sat with a straight spine. "I'm twenty-two and Darren is twenty-one. I guess you could say he likes older women." She shrugged. "But he turns twenty-two in a couple weeks."

Astonished, America wondered what they drink in the deep south that caused this couple to look so young, considering she herself was only a couple of years on from them. "Tell me how you met."

Brittney-Lynn looked at Darren and side-nodded indicating he should answer this one. America could appreciate the couple's non-verbal communication style, as it was a skill she and Leo had perfected during recent months. They so often worked in front of the guests at The Foundry and had found a way to say much without saying anything at all. Most couples, especially those who had been together the longest, like her own parents, seemed to have some level of telepathic ability.

"When she says she's been waiting her whole life, she is not exaggerating. We've known each other our whole lives. Our moms were in a bible study together back home—"

"And where is home?" America interrupted.

"Biloxi," Brittney-Lynn said.

"Mississippi," Darren added. "It wasn't love at first sight, but when she came back from summer break between sophomore and junior year of high school, looking the way she looks, my seventeen-year-old brain stopped seeing her as the girl I used to tease at church and saw her as someone I knew I had to have in my life."

"It took him another year to ask me out," Brittney-Lynn joked, and the couple gazed into each other's eyes.

"So, tomorrow is Valentine's Day. What made you pick this date for your nuptials?" America asked.

"Truth is, we were having a hard time picking a day. The more we sat on it, the more it seemed like everyone in our families—"

"And all our friends," Darren finished.

"Everyone had a different idea about what kind of wedding we were supposed to have," Brittney-Lynn said and sat back into the seat cushion. The annoyance at the turmoil of choosing a date was still written all over her pinched face. "So, I was at work. I'm a teller at the Beau Rivage Casino. Everyone I know pretty much works there. Anyway, I saw a flyer about Las Vegas trying to break the record for most weddings performed in one day. And I thought how perfect it sounded to be a part of something so fun. Nothing like this ever happens at home."

"If there's one piece of advice you can give other couples going through similar hardships as they navigate wedding planning, what would it be?" America asked.

They were both quiet for a minute and America waited patiently. Finally, Brittney-Lynn spoke. "I'd say to other couples that they should not let the wedding day define their marriage. A wedding is just a day, but the marriage is for a lifetime. We chose this path because it was the only way to stop everyone's bickering, and we thought it would be fun. It's not like anyone remembers the wedding really, so I don't know why they all care so much."

"We have a few close friends in town for the ceremony tomorrow, and we'll have a big party when we get home to celebrate with everyone else," Darren said.

America was falling in love with these two.

"It's said that what happens in Vegas stays in Vegas. In this case, what do you have to say about having such a public wedding that the whole world will know about."

"We think it's pretty cool. When we're old and sitting on the front porch with grandkids running around, we'll have a great story to tell," Darren said and winked at Brittney-Lynn.

"Can I just say something?" Brittney-Lynn said, and America nodded for her to continue. She looked at Darren. "Thank you for asking me out on the date and taking me to The Shed." She turned her attention back to America. "It's my favorite restaurant." With the clarifying over with, she turned back to Darren, "Thank you for getting up on that stage and taking the mic away from Max Foly who was in the middle of his set and fuming at you, and telling the entire crowd that you loved me and wanted to marry me." She wiped away a tear and kissed Darren on the tip of his nose. "I thought you were crazy, but now I know it was easier for you to show me how you really felt than keep it bottled up for one more day. I can't wait to start our lives together tomorrow."

"I love you so much," Darren said and took her cheeks between his hands to kiss her.

America tensed at seeing such a public display. Though she and Leo were known for spontaneous displays of affection too, she was not usually in the position to witness others. She cleared her throat, and the couple broke their bond. America switched the recorder off so that they could see.

"We're off the record now. Can I ask you both something? I'm about to get married next week and I feel like all we've done is make decisions that will make all of our friends and family happy, though there hasn't been bickering like you said. How did you do it?" America sat back in her chair.

Darren shrugged in the same way Leo does when he has something to say but won't.

"We just kept talking about what we wanted. We ignored the

opinions best we could and kept our eye on the ball. It was hard, but we told everyone about our plans to come to Vegas and just asked that they show us as much love and respect as we have always shown to them."

"And never underestimate the power of a southern girl with the tact of a mixed martial arts fighter and the voice of an angel," Darren laughed. "Congratulations are in order for you, too."

"I appreciate that. I'm rooting for you two." America thanked them for their time and showed them out.

What a powerful statement from the young couple. America could stand to learn a thing or two from Brittney-Lynn. She wished that she had the same level of clarity when it came to what she wanted. Ever since she and Leo had picked their date, she had done everything she could to make the wedding perfect for everyone. She did not want to let down the very people who had given her so much love and encouragement over the past year. But she knew she had compromised on many things.

December was her dream time of year to get married, but everyone in town had an opinion. Too close to Christmas, people were traveling, holiday festivals and busy social calendars. No one does anything in January but hibernate and recover from the holidays. Valentine's Day would have been perfect, but Leo said there was too much pressure on that day, so they had picked the following Saturday instead.

America paced the ballroom floor, following the grid lines created within the intricate woven design, and supposed the compromising had begun early in the process. She would have married him sooner, if not for renovating a house, helping Leo start and open a resort on the old lake, traveling every few weeks for work, and helping her mom with creating the boutique shop of her dreams. Her year had been packed with new adventures, and planning the wedding on top of everything else seemed like the only way to get to the good part; marrying Leopold Thorpe.

The next couple walked into the ballroom hand in hand and

made straight for her. She flipped her notebook to a fresh page and prepared for another interview. There were three planned in total. Afterwards, America would be free to walk the city and take in the sights. *For research purposes*, she told herself.

CHAPTER 4

Leo stood in front of the tall mirror hanging on the wall beside the hotel door and straightened his floral bow tie. His navy suit was crisp and clean with a pale blue button-down underneath. He thought he might be too hot but as it turned out, Las Vegas was freezing in February. Not only was the weather cold, but the lack of humidity in the air had his normally wavy blond hair looking more like a frizz ball on top of his head instead of the sexy tousled I-didn't-try-too-hard style he normally sported. He took one more pass, using hair wax this time, and calmed the mess into submission.

Walking down the hallway to America's room, Leo had a little pick-up in his step. Either from excitement or nerves, he wasn't sure, but he knew he couldn't wait to see his love. They had only been apart for a couple of days, but Leo missed her like he was missing a piece of himself. In all the times she had traveled for work since they were a couple, he had never surprised her on a work trip before. The idea wasn't even his. Cam had suggested the romantic gesture since Valentine's Day was coming up and America would be out of town on the day. The excuse sounded good enough to him, and he booked a flight.

At America's door, the sticky-note he had placed there earlier had been removed, hopefully by her or the next few minutes might prove to be awkward. He knocked and rehearsed his words in his mind. *Roses are red, violets are blue, you are everything to me, and I'm here for you.*

Only, when the door cracked open and America's long dark hair swung into the view between the door and the jamb, "Surprise!" is all that actually came out of his mouth. "Idiot," he chastised himself under his breath as she unlatched the door chain.

"Leo? What are you doing here?" America jumped at him through the half-open door.

Leo wrapped his arms around her waist and held her warm body against his. He buried his face in her hair. She smelled like heaven, amber and spice. "I wanted to surprise you. I had a whole thing worked out what I would say."

America planted her lips on his, cutting off his words and taking his breath away. Her lips tasted of mint and chocolate and felt delicious against his. Her silky dress clung to her body and Leo realized he needed to stop things now or they would never get to dinner. He unhooked her arms from around his neck and stood back, breathless. Her broad smile showed him how happy she was that he was there, and the sway of her hips told him he couldn't wait to marry this woman.

"I see you got my note." Leo took her hand above her head and twirled her around. Her red dress was perfect for what he had planned for the evening. "Gorgeous."

"The note said to be ready for a night on the town, and now that I know it was you who put the note on my door, you're up to something," she said with a raised brow and walked back inside the room fully. "I just need to get my bag. Where are we going, anyway?"

"We have a reservation," he checked his watch, "and we should hurry." Leo took her by the hand and led her down the hallway.

America tugged for him to slow down a little. "I can't walk this fast in these heels." She stopped and kicked up one of her feet towards her bum and he saw why. The shoes looked like diamond covered torture devices with tiny traps holding her foot into the sole all attached to the skinniest looking high heel he had ever seen.

"Nice. Are they new?" he asked.

"I'm breaking in my wedding heels," she winked, and he swallowed hard imagining what else she was planning on wearing next week.

It didn't take long to walk across the property to the Eiffel Tower elevator where a maître d' stood waiting for them. Upon their arrival at the elevator doors, the man handed a single red rose to America. At the top of the elevator, a hostess handed another rose stem to America and pointed the way to the left. Leo took America's arm in the crook of his own.

Following the directions, they walked towards the expansive glass windows and stepped down three steps where America received a pink rose from a gesturing server pointing them to the right. Turning as indicated, the spraying fountains of the Bellagio filled the skyline, and lush burgundy velvet booths hugged the candlelit tables intimately. A woman stood from her own seat at one of the tables and handed America yet another rose, followed by a man who did the same. By the time they arrived at their own table, America had amassed a bouquet of fourteen stems of various shades of red and pink.

America's mouth was agape, and her eyes were wide and blinking.

"One for each month I've known you," Leo said and kissed her nose.

A server pulled out a golden chair and Leo helped America around the square corner of the table. He sat across from her and felt her foot press against the inside of his ankle, something she did to ground herself. He smoothed the white clothed surface and watched her take in the moment.

America stared out at the view. "It's beautiful up here. You can see the whole strip. And look," she pointed with the enthusiasm of a little girl, "I didn't realize the water sprayed up that high. It's incredible. I bet the folks staying at that hotel don't know that this is probably the better viewing spot."

Leo fell in love with her every time she laughed, and this was no exception. If nothing else, the night was already worth the traveling and the cost. Though he was sure his credit card was near maxed from all the last-minute wedding expenses. At least The Foundry, the resort he and America had opened nine months ago, had its own line of accounting.

She turned back to him, after thoroughly taking in the water and lights show. "What should we order?" she said. "I'm starving."

"I hope you don't mind, but I pre-ordered. There were only three choices, seeing as it's Valentine's weekend." The server appeared and poured two large wine glasses with about an inch of red wine. "Everything is taken care of. We can just enjoy the meal."

"You're amazing. I was missing you terribly today with all this wedding stuff. I thought I was the ideal person to cover this story, seeing as how our wedding is coming up. That's the only reason I agreed to this assignment in the first place." America sipped her wine. "I just didn't think it would be so emotional seeing all the couples getting married tomorrow and trying on my dress this morning…"

"That's right. How did the fitting go?" Leo asked.

"It was good. A little bit lonely though. There was a… mishap with some of the beading and I have to go back tomorrow to pick it up. Jenny texted me to see how things were going." She paused. "Wait, did she know about this?"

Leo shrugged like he knew nothing about it, but the truth was clearly visible on his smirking face. "I would have checked in with you, but I was sort of in the air at the time."

"Wait a—How did you? When did you plan all this?" America said with her half smile pulling up more on one side than the other.

The candlelight danced in her sable eyes, and he reached for her hand across the table. "I wanted you to have a special time, since last Valentine's Day was a disaster."

"It wasn't that bad…"

"We were knee-deep in whatever had been rotting underneath the barn's floorboards for a hundred years." He laughed at the memory. "By the time we dug ourselves out, I don't think either of us was in the mood for a romantic night out."

"A hot shower was all I wanted after that!" America took a long breath. "You didn't have to come here and surprise me, but I'm so glad you did. This is exactly what I needed."

Leo had always wanted a love like his parents had. Even though they had passed away years ago, he could sense that they would be happy for him and America. So far, everything had come together with few problems. America had planned the perfect wedding day with the help of practically the whole town. She complained about nothing and always had a smile on her face, which is why the pinched brow she now sported concerned him.

"What is it? Too much?"

"No." she shook her head. "I just don't know what I did to deserve this. You."

Leo chuckled. "I could list all the reasons. Or I could just say that I love you America Greene—almost Thorpe—and that should be enough."

"I love you too," America said and held up her flowers. "What should I do with these?"

As if on cue, a server appeared with a slender vase and placed it at the center of the table. The man, dressed in black pants, a white button down, and a red tie, took the stems and propped them up inside the smooth glass cylinder, which completely obscured their view of one another. Leo leaned towards the window on his left. "We could just look outside the whole time."

"Fine with me. The view is pretty good," she giggled but moved the vase to one side anyway. "Better?"

After dinner, they bundled up and walked the strip, taking in the street performers, and dodging the people on every corner, passing out what looked to be baseball cards, which instead of hunky athletes, featured beautiful women wearing next to nothing. In front of the fountains, a man played a violin better than any performer Leo had ever heard.

The sounds vibrated through the air like a dreamy lullaby, and there was only one thing to do. "May I have this dance?" he asked and spun America away from his body. When she nodded, he pulled her back in towards himself.

Colliding, she looked up at him. A contented smile softened the lower half of her face. "You may have this dance, and the next, and every dance for the rest of our lives, Leopold Thorpe."

CHAPTER 5

The next morning, as America waited in the lobby for Leo to arrive, she couldn't help but play the events of last night through her mind. Her heart flittered just thinking about the most magical date she had ever been on. She weighed the date against the next best moment of her life when Leo proposed at midnight on Christmas Eve while the snow fell around them. That night, too, had been a surprise, but never in a million years did she think Leo would sweep her off her feet so unexpectedly in Las Vegas.

Dinner at the Eiffel Tower restaurant had been delicious, and she could still recall the taste of that nutty mountain cheese, Comté, and the fresh baked bread that had practically melted in her mouth. After dinner, they had danced in the shadow of the fountain light show at the Bellagio hotel to the most beautiful violin music. Later, they had shared a scoop of pistachio gelato beneath the glow of the Las Vegas Sphere which had quite literally been displaying the night sky like a reverse planetarium. When they kissed while riding to the top of the largest ferris wheel she'd ever been on, she had totally forgotten about how cold she was.

The thrill of last night still warmed her through and through. But now, as she checked her watch and wondered where the heck Leo was and why he was late, irritation built in her stomach. She tapped her pointy toe on the tile floor of the lobby and watched the couples who were there for the big ceremony begin to congregate.

"Sorry, I'm late," Leo said as he startled her from behind, with his hands clasping her shoulders.

America turned and kissed him quickly on his lips. "It's fine. I'm just a little nervous."

"Why? It's not like you're the one getting married today," Leo joked.

"You're right. Take a breath, America," she said to herself out loud, the way she had learned to do to calm down. There was power in saying things aloud that the human brain tended to listen to better than just saying things in one's head. She sucked cool air, chilled by the constantly opening and closing lobby doors, in through her nostrils.

"You good to go in?" Leo asked. "I'm excited to be part of this, or at least witness it. How did you get me a place inside anyway?"

"I called Margarete, the manager, and told her all about you. You'd think she would have had enough of hearing people's sappy love stories this week, with all the couples in town for the mass wedding today, but she lapped up our story."

America took Leo's arm, and they walked through the ringing bells and flashing lights of the casino on their way to the conference center at the east end. The hallways were crowded with couples of all shapes, sizes, ages, and cultures. America was surprised to see so many people wearing traditional wedding attire from all over the world. She wanted to snap photos but was told the official photographer would distribute the images directly to the magazine. America committed the sight to memory for writing's sake, and escorted Leo to the ballroom where she had held the interviews yesterday.

At a registration table a tall, thin man stopped them. "Name please," he said.

"Oh, we're not here to get married," she said. "I'm a journalist, and this is my fiancé—"

"Name."

"America Greene," she said.

"Leopold Thorpe," Leo said and shrugged at her.

"Thank you," the man said. "You may go in."

Once inside, they had a good laugh about it. "Is your job always so intense?" Leo asked.

"Not usually, though I did try to save a town once." she winked.

"That didn't go so well, did it?"

He was referring to the time when they tried to save Christmas Cove from being incorporated by the next town over, and even though they failed, she knew that everyone had still come out ahead by the new arrangement, herself and Leo included. "I think we did alright."

"I think so too." Leo winked back at her.

Taking in the romantic space, Margarete had not understated the ballroom's transformation. From one end to the next, the space was dotted with pink and white floral arches that created little intimate areas for the couples to stand. Tulle swags hung from the center of the ceiling and draped to the outer walls. Sparkling twinkle-lights played with the tulle and pooled along the edges of the room. The over-the-top décor was to be expected from the city of love, even if that meant she was in Nevada and not France.

Margarete spotted America and waved her up to the main stage. America dragged Leo, who was busy investigating the room, up the stairs to the narrow platform covered in a maroon carpet. The backdrop of the entire scene consisted of yards and yards of pink and red velvet and tulle cascading from an overhead structure. Studio lighting and cameras hung from positions over head, and dozens of chandeliers were positioned on brass stands of varying heights. Light scattered around the ballroom like the mirrors of Versailles at sunset.

The room looked more spectacular from this new vantage point. "This is extraordinary," America said to Margarete as they kissed each other's cheeks.

Margarete took a turn gazing out at the room. "Do you think the brides will like it?"

"Absolutely," America said.

"And what about the grooms?" Leo acted offended.

"No one cares what the groom likes as long as he likes the bride," Margarete quipped and checked the time. "The press is positioned over there, but I thought you would like to be up here with some of the officials from town. It won't be long now. The couples are already filtering in."

Several double doors along the perimeter opened simultaneously. No sooner did the staff get out of the way, than the couples paraded in. Each stopped at a designated table at the entrances and presumably registered their attendance as America and Leo had been forced to do.

Margarete approached their location again with a short little man following close behind. "America, this is the official overseeing the count for the record bid," Margarete said.

America shook the man's hand, all the while a flashback of her first December in Christmas Cove played in her mind. Then, Leo had stood by as an official had performed a headcount of the town's population. That particular count had come up too short to make a difference, which led to Leo losing his job as the mayor. She only hoped this count would go the right way for the people gathered in the ballroom.

"Nice to meet you," America said. "I'm a journalist and writing a story about the city of love. Did you know that more marriages are performed in Las Vegas each year than anywhere else in the country? Would you like to give a quote for me to use in the article?"

He nodded and she pulled out her recorder. "State your name and that you agree to be recorded."

After he complied, he began. "As someone that counts things for a living, I'm thrilled to be the official presiding over today's attempt at the world record for most simultaneous marriages performed in America at one time, giving Las Vegas the undisputed title as the City of Love."

"Do you think they'll have it?"

"I can't give anything away, but it's looking like a good day to have a wedding." He nodded that he was done and thanked her before walking away.

The room was quickly filling to the max. Staff busied themselves with corralling couples to certain areas of the room. A paramedic and firefighter positioned themselves near one of the doors with an EXIT sign lit up in green above their heads. Margarete moved through the crowd with ease, greeting many of the couples.

"I should walk around and get some more sound bites," America said. "Will you hold our chairs? I'll be back in a few minutes."

America weaved between the couples, being careful not to step on any dress trains, or coattails. Every kind of dress imaginable was on full display, but the more people huddled together, the more stifling the room became and the harder it was for her to move amongst the people. She let her breathing normalize and spotted a rather unique looking couple, dressed in matching silver sequined suits from head to toe.

She approached them. "Hello, my name is America and I'm a journalist with Jet Trek Magazine. Can I ask you about your rather spectacular outfits?"

One of the men answered, "We met on New Years eve in Times Square. Fitting, isn't it?"

America agreed. "Six weeks ago? Why did you choose Las Vegas, and specifically this event, to make it official?"

"When you know, you know. Plus, what better place to get married than the city known for so many famous weddings?"

"Like Britney…"

"And Bennifer. Can't forget about them."

"Or Zach and Kelly."

"Zach and Kelly?" America stopped their listing.

"You know," the first man chuckled. "From *Saved by the Bell*."

"I don't know if you can count that one, it was just a show." America giggled along with them.

"Just a show?" one of them said and placed a hand over his wounded heart.

"I get it. You want your wedding to be in good company?"

"Absolutely, and with all these other beautiful people. Who wouldn't want to get married here, like this?"

Me, she thought, *that's who*. As fun as the event looked to be for the waiting couples, it wasn't the kind of wedding she would ever have wanted for herself. She thanked the couple for their time and congratulated them on their marriage.

Snaking her way through the room and talking to a few stand-out couples, the crush of bodies only intensified. She thought it was best she return to the stage and find Leo before getting lost in the sea of tulle and crystals. She arrived beside Leo just as the officiant entered the stage from the back side behind all the draping.

He tapped on the microphone and waited for the room to quiet. "Good morning to all of you beautiful, glowing brides and grooms here today. If everyone is finished registering, what do you say we begin?"

The people cheered and the sound was deafening. As the room stilled again, the lively atmosphere was replaced with one that felt more serious, as though each person present realized the magnitude of what was about to happen. Leo took America's hand and pulled it to his lap as they sat off to one end of the long stage. Even though she and Leo were a week away from their own wedding, the weight of their choice was in the air around them too. She looked down at the ring on her finger. The delicate lace setting and tiny stones fashioned in the shape of a snowflake reminded her of the reason she loved him so much. He had known her before really getting to know her, like their love was meant to be.

"We are gathered here today, to celebrate the joining of two souls in matrimony. As this is a civil ceremony, you will simply repeat after me. I, say your name, take you to be my lawfully wedded spouse."

The unison in which the group repeated was beautiful; a choir of people professing their love. So much tenderness could be heard in the way they emphasized certain syllables. She caught Leo mouthing the words. "Are you practicing?" she leaned over and whispered.

"Why not?" he said and ran his free hand through his blond hair.

The officiant continued, "Before these witnesses, I vow to love you... Care for you... And honor you all the days of our lives." When the couples finished, he said what everyone was waiting for. "You may now seal your union with a kiss."

Leo tugged America towards him. His eyes were full of love and maybe a tear, though he would never admit it, and he licked his lips. She knew what he wanted and leaned into him, shoulder to shoulder. She loved this man more than words could describe, which was a lot to say considering she was a writer for a living, but some things were indescribable.

America closed her eyes and felt the warmth of Leo's pillowy lips touch hers. She returned the kiss and just let their connection last, not wanting the delicious kiss to end. The room was theirs in that moment. She could have heard a pin drop but for the rustling of hundreds of taffeta skirts and crinolines. As the couples broke off their kissing, the noise loudened until all she and Leo could do was giggle through the clapping and cheers.

"I love you," America said, and Leo mouthed the words back to her. She was more excited than ever to marry this man in one week's time.

The couples all congratulated each other, and she and Leo stood and joined the applause from their little corner. Even the first responders celebrated, and she swore one of the men wiped a tear off his cheek. The enthusiasm was palpable, like the hearts of all the people present beat in time with one another.

Several minutes went by before the representative from Guinness came to the mic. "Congratulations. I know you're ready to begin your honeymoons but first we have to tabulate the official results. As you know, the current record was set in 2019 in New York City in honor of the city's new *I heart NY* campaign. If you're successful here today, with a total of four thousand and two couples, then Las Vegas Nevada will hold the record as America's city of love."

A woman walked from the set of double doors at the far side and made her way through the anticipating crowd, some still embracing while others danced to the soft ambient music playing throughout the ballroom. She handed over an envelope, but her smile gave it away before he opened the flap and retrieved the results.

He leaned into the mic, and it screeched. Backing off, he began. "Well, folks, it looks like you've done it!" He was forced to talk over the top of the cheering couples. "With a total of four thousand and two couples taking their vows simultaneously, Las Vegas has won it. Congratulations for being in the history books!"

America was overwhelmed from experiencing the shared joyous occasion and squeezed Leo's hand in hers.

Margarete hung her arms over the back of America and Leo's

shoulders and nestled her head between theirs. "Congratulations, you two. I didn't know you were getting married today."

"Come again?" Leo bolted from his chair and left America's hand floating in midair.

"I was surprised to see your names in the registry," she kissed America's cheeks. "I'm thrilled for you both. Simply thrilled."

"I... I um, think you made a mistake. We're getting married next week. Next Saturday. Not today." America stumbled as her mind caught up.

Margarete's face deflated. "Are you certain?"

"I'm pretty sure our wedding is next week on the other side of the country. Not here," Leo said and kicked the invisible dirt on the ground. "And not today."

"Margarete, there must be some mistake. I don't know how they would have counted us..." America scratched her head while Margarete called the representative over to join them.

"Is there a problem here?" he asked.

Margarete spoke into a walkie talkie and instructed the staff to hold the doors for a moment. "Tell him what you told me."

America cleared her throat and Leo stepped in. "We didn't get married today, though somehow, we were counted."

The man flipped through the registry print out and Margarete pointed at the pages. "Thorpe and Greene?"

Leo nodded and America gripped his hand like she was about to pull an emergency brake.

"It looks like you did get married today. Congratulations," he said.

How could this happen? America replayed the whole morning in her mind and snapped her fingers. "When we came in this morning, a man," she scanned the room and pointed at the tall man sitting behind a table, "that man took our names. Do you think he thought..."

"That you two were participating? I dare say so." The man held up the list and pointed to their names. "But if you're saying it was a mistake, I regret that I'll have to withhold the record from all these soon-to-be unhappy couples, until we can get this figured out."

"You mean…" The reality was sinking in. America took both of Leo's hands and gauged his thoughts. Was he thinking what she was thinking? How could they accidentally get married? In Vegas, no less! As irritation traveled up her throat along with her breakfast, she caught a glimpse of all the waiting couples in the ballroom. "All these people, what do we do?"

"I did say my vows today, just like all of them did," Leo said with a wink.

She cracked a smile and bit her lower lip as the truth set in. "So did I."

Leo kissed her lightly on the mouth. "Does this mean we're—"

"Husband and wife? I think so. If we want to be." It's not that America wasn't prepared to marry this man, but for all the sleepless nights and stress of planning the perfect wedding, this was not how things were supposed to go. America turned to Margarete. "We don't have a license or anything though."

"The Clark County Registrar is here with a pop-up office, I believe they are still processing all the registrations and certificates right now, we can slip yours in. Is that sufficient?" she asked the official. "It's your call."

"I don't see any issue so long as you both agree, and I'll keep all of this hush hush," he answered. "Just get that paperwork done so that I don't have to deal with four thousand angry brides."

"Understood," Leo said and took America in his arms. Pressing a more passionate kiss to her lips, he hugged her body tightly to his. She could feel his muscles flex around her in an unfamiliar way, like he was using the kiss to expel his anxiety. "Mrs. Thorpe," he whispered between kisses, and the sound of her new name rolling off his tongue sent chills through her.

Whether she was ready or not, she was his now.

CHAPTER 6

The tip of the ballpoint pen scraped across the paper with the final flick of Leo's signature. He dropped the pen and slid the document back to the registrar.

After looking it over, the expressionless older woman slid a pair of driver's licenses back to Leo. "Congratulations on your wedding," she said like she was numb to the excitement still filling the ballroom and squeezed a brass seal against the corner of the license. "Check your mail in ten to thirty days for your copy. Have a nice day. NEXT!"

With America's fingers intertwined with his, they walked out through the ballroom doors and laughed once they were out of earshot of the registrar. "I can't believe we just did that." Leo stopped and pulled America in for a hug. The whole moment seemed like a dream. America looked up at him with shiny eyes. "What's troubling you?"

"Is it bad that I'm not feeling happier?" she shook her head at her own question. "What are we going to do about the wedding next week?"

"Listen to me, America. You are allowed to feel however you want. I won't lie and say I know how you're feeling. I think it's pretty cool that we just got married and helped all these other couples make it into the history books."

"I don't mean I'm not happy to be married to you." America shook her head and looked down at the ground. "Of course, I want to marry you, it just doesn't feel real."

He tilted her chin back and straightened her shoulders. "I hate to break it to you, but we *are* married."

America slapped his upper arm and grunted. "Don't tease me."

"You like it when I tease you," Leo moved a stray tendril behind her ear. "As for the wedding next week, why don't we just call everyone and tell them what happened. They'll probably all have a good laugh at this."

America stood back from him with a look of disgust wrinkling her face. "You can't be serious. We'd be letting everyone down. And all that waste... It makes me sick thinking about it. Oh goodness, here comes Margarete. How's my face?"

"Fine?" Leo said, not knowing how to answer the question, though he suspected there was no correct response. "I'll take care of this." He closed the distance and greeted Margarete in the vestibule outside the ballroom where other couples were still making their way out.

"I am just delighted for you both. What a special way to begin your forever together." Margarete kissed him on both cheeks. "Did you ever imagine?"

America caught up and shook her head, no. Leo nudged her in the shoulder, and she threw a smile on her beautiful face. "We couldn't have planned it better if we'd tried."

"Well, America, Leopold, on behalf of Paris Resort and Casino, we want to gift you with the penthouse room tonight and reservations in the tower—"

"That's very kind," America interrupted.

"On one condition. You must include your story in the article about this City of Love." Margarete beamed.

"I appreciate the offer, but we can't stay. We're flying out this afternoon." At that statement, America checked her watch. "Shoot. I'm running late already."

"To the airport?" Leo asked.

"No. I'm supposed to pick up my wedding dress from alterations. Not that I need it anymore."

Leo's heart broke at how sad the words sounded as they spilled from her mouth. What should have been a joyous occasion was tinged with her concern that all her work planning a wedding was now a waste. It was as though she was mourning the loss of having her dream wedding that she had been meticulously planning for months. He couldn't begin to try and understand what the big deal was, but he knew if it meant so much to her, he should at least seem sympathetic.

"We'll pick up your dress and then head over to the airport. I know you just want to get home. How's that sound for a plan?" Leo asked, and she nodded. "We can talk about how we want to handle all the wedding stuff while we're on the plane. That's a few hours, just me and you. No distractions." America was silent but nodded, and Leo was sure he saw a slight one-sided grin. Taking her hand, he addressed Margarete's offer. "Can we have a raincheck?"

"You are welcome to visit Paris anytime as honored guests. I'll leave you to it. Have a good journey home and congratulations again." She kissed America on both cheeks. "You are a beautiful bride, and I'm happy to have met you."

"Thank you, Margarete, for everything," America said and led the way to her suite.

Though the walk and elevator ride were taken in silence, her grip on his hand said it all. She was stressing about the wedding, and Leo couldn't stop himself from seeing this rocky, unexpected beginning of their marriage as a bad omen. What did it matter what day the official records say the union took place on? This Saturday, or next, it made no difference to him. The whole point was to marry the stunning woman to his left.

She was upset and hiding her feelings poorly. Leo didn't know why she was so bothered, but he figured they had several hours to sort it out before making it back to Christmas Cove by evening. He wanted nothing more than to have a love as strong as the one his parents shared before they passed away, and he thought he had found that with America. He just hoped this accidental wedding wasn't ruining everything.

He reminded himself that a single day does not make a whole marriage as they stopped at his hotel room door. "I'll grab my things and meet you in your room in a few minutes." Leo kissed her on the tip of the nose. "Everything is going to be fine. I love you."

"I love you too." America gave him a hug and whispered, "husband," in his ear. She turned and walked down the hall to her nearby room, looking back at him over her shoulder with a sly grin on her face. He knew in that tiny flexing of facial muscles, that they would be alright when the dust kicked up by the unexpected events of the morning finally settled.

Leo waited outside his door until she reached hers and they opened their doors at the same time. Their eyes stayed locked onto one another's as they entered their respective suites. As the door closed behind him, Leo took one more look at the Eiffel Tower positioned outside his room's window. The sun shined on the tower's polished surface and reflected streaks of light in through the window and across the far wall. His bag was already packed, save for the gift he had planned to give to America for Valentine's Day. Though the small heart shaped box of chocolates was nice for a romantic holiday, it lacked the luster that she deserved on a wedding day. He shoved it inside the weekender bag and double checked the bathroom for loose items.

His phone buzzed in his pants pocket. He read the message from the airline and immediately headed to America's room. Out in the hallway, America stepped out of her room and held up her phone towards him. "Canceled?" they said at the same time.

Leo clicked the link and a text box popped up in a blue square on the screen. He read it out loud. "Attention: Due to inclement weather impacting your area, your flight has been canceled. Chat with a representative now."

"What weather?" America said and pointed out to the sun-washed skyline.

Leo opened the weather app and waited for the radar image to load. "It looks like there's a huge storm, a bomb cyclone or something. Take a look. It stretches from Colorado to the Great Lakes and is moving towards home. I doubt any flights are going that way. Why don't you finish packing and I'll chat with the airline and see what our options are."

It didn't take long for the representative to inform him that the next available flight out of Vegas to anywhere in the Northeast wouldn't be until Friday at the earliest.

"How do you feel about taking Margarete up on her offer to stay here?" Leo said. "We can't get a flight home until Friday."

"Friday!" America said from the bathroom where it sounded like she was rearranging pots and pans and not throwing a few plastic toiletries into a bag. "That's a whole week. What are we supposed to do?"

"Hide out in Vegas and ignore the fact that we have to tell everyone coming to our wedding that we accidently got married already?"

"You're not funny, Leopold Thorpe."

"Yes, I am, America Thorpe. But why shouldn't we have our honeymoon here?"

She poked her head out of the door and glared at him. "We can't just ignore the fact that we're getting married next Saturday, and everyone is counting on us." She ducked back inside the bathroom, and he heard the metal shower hooks scrape along the curtain bar. "How long is it to drive home? Two days?"

"Maybe, if we drove all day and all night." Leo checked the

map app, and it showed three different routes. "The fastest route would bring us straight through the bad weather, so if we go the southern way, it'll take us four days at best."

"Sounds better than waiting here and driving myself crazy losing all sense of control over this wedding fiasco."

"Really? Staying here and lounging in a beautiful hotel room with my new bride for a few days, sounds like heaven to me," Leo said.

America came out of the bathroom, ignoring his reasoning, wearing light blue jeans and a white tee. She had twisted her long, dark hair into a knot on top of her head the way he liked so that he could see the length of her neck. She smiled at his smile. "When can we leave?"

"After I kiss you properly," Leo said, settling for a single moment since the question of staying at the hotel and waiting for a flight seemed resolved for the time being.

He wrapped his fingers around her waist and used his grip to pull her against his body. Her hand rested on his chest as she bit her lower lip. There was no need to say anything. Without an audience or prying eyes, he was free to show her how happy he was that she was now his wife.

America arched up on her toes and their lips touched, sending little shocks through his body. As they joined in a passionate kiss, heat traveled up his neck and to the tips of his fingers. She was pliable in his arms and let out a little moan as he flicked his tongue gently against hers. The kiss was everything he needed to belay his own concerns. She loved him, he was sure the rest would work itself out.

She was the first to pull away. "Let's get going."

"I'll get a rental car," Leo said. This road trip was happening whether he wanted it to or not. "If we leave now, we should be able to get to the Colorado border tonight."

CHAPTER 7

America looked out the windshield of the rented Range Rover and spotted Leo walking into the gas station. She had put him on snack duty while she was on call-home-and-explain duty. Talking to Carol would be easy. As the woman that kept Christmas Cove together, Carol knew everything about everything. People knew it was better to just tell her things up front and save the trouble of having to dig out of a hole later. Calling her parents was something America wished to avoid for as long as possible and was relieved that they were unreachable on a cruise for a few more days.

After a few rings, Carol answered. "America, is that you? You're back already?"

"Hi, Carol. There's been a change of plans, and I needed to let you know something." America hesitated, not wanting to let down the woman who had become like a grandmother to her over the past year. "Leo flew out to Las Vegas to surprise me for Valentine's Day, and well…" she paused not knowing how to say the thing that she didn't quite believe herself.

Carol cleared her throat in the silence. "This sounds ominous. Is everything okay?"

"No. I mean to say, that we are both fine. Good, even. But we accidentally…"

"Is this about the wedding?" Carol hid a giggle in her throat. "You're not getting cold feet, are you? The whole town is buzzing about the big day."

"They are?" America knew they were, but hearing Carol admit it made it sound truer.

It was also true that the news of the wedding had brought more joy and excitement to the village than any other event had all year, except when the heavy spring rain added to the snowmelt and temporarily refilled the cove. It had been dried up for so long, people forgot what it felt like to dive in, swim, float, and splash. Now, with the wedding rapidly approaching in only one week's time, and excitement building, she didn't have it in her to tell Carol the truth yet.

"Our flight got canceled, and we decided to drive home. It'll take a few days, but the earliest they could reschedule our flight was going to be Friday. This way, we should roll back to town Tuesday some time. There's still so much to do and I don't want to waste the week away."

"Well, we can help out, if you need anything in the meantime. Where are you now? Still in Vegas?"

"We're at a stop somewhere in Utah already," America said. "Scrubby bushes and red dirt, that's all I see around here."

"Missing the Cove?" Carol said.

"You know I am."

"So, you need me to help out with some of the last-minute items before the wedding. I am the maid of honor and it's my duty to help the bride in a time of need."

Not having considered a charade as a viable option, it now seemed like a ruse might work out after all. No one would need to know that she and Leo were already married. It was the church and the ceremony, and the reception with all their favorite people around, that mattered most. America would worry about the guilt of lying to everyone later.

"Carol, you're a life saver. Well, a wedding saver maybe."

"What's in your planner for the next couple days?"

From her tote, America pulled out her wedding planning book. She opened the peony-covered cover and flipped to the calendar section. She scrolled the page with her finger. "Monday is the final menu selection at The Foundry with Alfonso. Tuesday is the day I was supposed to select the fresh flowers with Thandie. And on Wednesday, I should be able to make it in time for your dress fitting. I don't want to miss it."

"If you're not back yet, I'll just make Edwin come with me." Carol laughed, and America pictured Carol dragging the old soldier around town doing the most girly things. "Other than that, consider it handled. You just concentrate on getting home safely. We'll all do what we can here in the meantime."

"I have no doubt you'll do a great job. I appreciate it, and make sure to be careful. Apparently, there's some big storm heading your way. That's why all the flights heading east were canceled." America saw Leo exit the little trading post with a big smile splashed across his face, and she wondered what had put him in such a cheerful mood. "I need to let you go, but just call me if you have any questions. And don't be too worried if you can't reach me for a stretch, we're pretty much in no man's land right now." Leo opened the driver's door and climbed in. America held up a finger and finished her call. "Thanks Carol. Talk soon."

Leo passed her a chilled bottle of Dr. Pepper and a bag of her favorite sour cream and onion flavored chips. "I think I succeeded with my snack task. How did Carol take the news?"

"She's fine with it," America said.

"She wasn't too shocked?"

"Well…" America cranked open the bottle lid and took a swig. The spicy bubbles sank down her throat and gave her a moment to word the next part just right. "I was about to tell her everything about the wedding being off, but she was so excited and said that everyone is looking forward to it so much. I couldn't let her down and break her heart. I told her our flights were canceled and that we won't be back to town until Tuesday at the soonest. So, she asked how she can help us move things along with the wedding and I decided there's no harm in going ahead with the ceremony and party. I think we'll regret not celebrating with the people we love."

"I'm on board if you're certain. So long as nothing else goes wrong," Leo said.

"It's settled then. We just pretend like nothing happened this morning."

"Do we have to pretend about all of it?" Leo smirked.

"How about we just get to the hotel. Where are we staying tonight anyway?" America pulled out a cheap tourist map that she picked up at the car rental place and unfolded the half dozen sections. "It looks like there's nothing from here to the other side of the Rockies."

"The guy inside said there's a place a couple hours from here near Four Corners. He said there would be signs when we get closer. You might not like it though."

"Leo? Why won't I like it?" She buckled her seat belt. "Where are you taking me?"

"He said it's a little rustic, but it's either this, or drive another few hours," Leo said and pressed the ignition button on the center console. Pressing it again, nothing happened.

"What's the matter?" America asked, though it was clear the car wasn't starting.

"Jeez, I don't know, America. The car won't start for some reason." Leo snapped his answer.

"Well, I didn't do it. Don't take it out on me."

Leo pulled out his phone and typed something into the rental car chat app, while America popped open the glove compartment. A laminated trifold card sat right on top, with the word 'Troubleshooting' typed across the front. She opened it and skimmed the page.

"Leo, is the car in park?"

"Of course, it is," he said sharply, and checked the shifter buttons anyway. "Well, no." Leo pressed the P button and tried the ignition again. The engine started like it was supposed to. "Sorry," Leo said with a sheepish crack to his tone. "I guess I had already shifted to drive before hitting the ignition. I didn't mean to snap at you. I guess I'm feeling the stress of this drive more than I thought."

"I'm just glad we can get on our way. The last thing we need is another delay," America said with a sigh of relief as Leo pulled out from underneath the shade of the gas station roof.

For February, the desert sun was unforgiving. Though the temperature outside was cold, the rays poured through the windshield and heated the air inside the glass. Outside, dry wind whistled across the barren land and looked nothing like winter should. Cold, and cozy, and blanketed in white, that's what winters are for.

The highway snaked out in front of them and dipped into a gulch-like canyon in the distance. The landscape of southern Utah consisted of rolling hills stained red with ancient rust. Small round bushes, gray from winter, carpeted the ground like sad little monuments to the harshness of life there. The scenery was so unlike home with its tall green pines and flocked split-rail fences that America would give anything to see a snowflake or two.

The hours passed by quickly, and slowly at the same time. There was little differentiation from one mile to the next, red earth, little greenery, and towering mesas on the horizon. The landscape lulled her into a daydream. America found herself picturing the date night she shared with Leo in Vegas, between one mile marker and another. Even though it was only last night, so much had happened that the moment felt remote in her mind, like it had all been a wonderful illusion.

Needing to feel her husband and ground herself in reality, she laced her fingers with Leo's where their arms rested on the console between the two front seats. When she finally saw the brown road-sign indicating lodging ahead, she checked the map to see exactly where they were. Leo followed the signs to where the road split off from the sleek blacktop highway and turned into a red dirt road heading north.

He paused at the intersection and looked at her. "It'll be fine. Nothing to worry about."

"Convincing me, or you?" she giggled. "Like you said, it'll be fine. Let's just go see what it is."

They traveled down the road for about a mile and crested over a small hill. Dozens of rustic structures came into view and a few RVs were parked in the shade of the only trees she had seen for an hour or more. "It's like an oasis or something."

Leo pulled up to the front of the only log style cabin in sight. A welcome sign, affixed above a small, covered porch indicated where to park. Leo was the first out and came around to open her door. She hopped down from her high position and shielded her eyes from the sun hanging low in the sky. On the porch, an empty rocking chair moved by its own volition and tumbleweed rolled past her feet. "Nothing to worry about, huh?"

Walking through the saloon style door was like walking back in time to the wild west. A long, polished wood countertop stretched along one side. Behind the counter, shelves overflowed with essential, yet modern, items from canned goods to band-aids. Seeing no employees, America dinged the brass desk bell sitting at the closest corner of the counter.

"Hello?" she called out without having waited for anyone to answer the bell's ding and turned back towards the doors. "I guess no one's here. We should just get back in the car and keep going."

It was Leo's turn to laugh. "Let's just see what—"

"Good evening, weary travelers," a man said as he came out from a back room. "You need somewhere to stay the night?" he laughed, though America was unsure what was funny. "Just a joke. No one comes out here unless they need a place to sleep. I have the market cornered. It's either this or whatever horse you came in on. Do you need a hook-up for a recreational vehicle, or do you need a hogan?"

"A what-an?"

"A hogan. It's a traditional dwelling of the Navajo people. You're not from around here, are you?"

"Is anyone?" Leo said.

"That's rude," the man with dark black hair said and turned to leave. "I'm just messing with you. This is tribal land, but even Navajo know better than to rough it in this harsh land nowadays."

Leo wiped the mortification off his face and forced a grin. "A hogan will be great. Thank you."

"Do you have one with two beds?" America asked and looked at Leo. In the year since being engaged, they hadn't been intimate yet. She had wanted to wait until their wedding night. Their real wedding night. "I know we technically got married today, but it doesn't feel right just yet."

"Married? Today? Congratulations," the man said. America and Leo nodded in unison. "But I'm afraid we only have rooms with one bed. King size, you can sleep on opposite ends if you need to, but I don't know many newlyweds who would do that."

America was officially embarrassed. "One bed is fine. Thank you."

Leo slapped his credit card on the counter. "Do you take AmEx?"

The man nodded and took Leo's card. "My name is Nahele. And let me know if I can make your stay any better." He handed over a metal room key attached to something that looked like a scrap of a two by four. "Number eight. Can't miss it, and you can park right in front of your unit."

Leo thanked the man and tucked America's shoulders under his arm as they walked out.

"There's a community bonfire at eight o'clock and breakfast is at sunrise at the circle."

After driving around a large circular road, Leo parked in front of the hogan numbered eight. They grabbed all of their luggage, including America's dress tucked away in the satin garment bag, and went inside. The eight-sided structure was made of sticks and packed mud, but inside, light from several windows lining the outer walls of the one room house flooded the space. In the center of the room, there was one king size bed with loads of white linens and plush pillows calling to America.

Wasting no time, she dropped the luggage and flopped down into the center of the mattress. The fluffy covers seemed to hug her. "It's almost as good as your beds back at The Foundry. Nahele is giving you a run for your money. You may be known in Christmas Cove for expertly made-up beds, but this one is pretty darn good."

"I'll take your word for it," Leo said and walked behind a bulkhead that acted as the bed's headboard and separated the bathroom area from the bedroom. He turned on the water and she could tell he was washing his hands. When he came back out, he looked longingly at the bed. "How am I so tired?"

America patted her hand on the covers beside her. "Come lay with me?"

"Are you sure it's not too soon?" His words were tinged with annoyance.

She turned to her side and looked at him. "I'm sorry, I didn't mean to sound hurtful, about the two beds. It's just…. I don't know."

"A lot to take in?"

She nodded because tears were pushing at her eyes.

Leo swept the tear from her upper cheek and kissed her lightly on her lips. "We can take as long as you need. We've waited for fourteen months... Let's just sleep. And attack tomorrow with everything we have."

She kissed him back. "Thank you for understanding."

CHAPTER 8

It may not have been the wedding night he had imagined. Waking up beside his very clothed wife, Leo still felt like he was dreaming the whole thing from getting married in Vegas to deciding to road trip across the country. Outside, the first light of day reflected off of the rusty earth and cast the whole room in an amber hue. America's rosy cheeks and luscious lips begged to be peppered with little kisses. Her warm skin greeted his lips and her eyes fluttered open. "Morning," he whispered.

America pulled her covers up over her chin and mouth, but he could see she was smiling under the thin white sheet. "What time is it?" The fabric muffled her words.

"Nearly seven. We should get on the road before too long," he said and pulled the sheet down, exposing her smile and dark lashes. "You're beautiful in the morning. Have I ever told you that?"

"You've seen me in the morning before," America said and sat up. The covers fell away from her red and pink plaid pajamas, that covered way too much skin for his liking, but were completely appropriate for the cool desert winter temperatures.

"Maybe so, but I've never woken up in the same bed as you,

and I've certainly never roused you with kisses before." Leo leaned in and America rewarded him with a sweet peck. "You want to get breakfast before we go?"

"I could eat a horse," she said, and Leo knew better than to let her get overly-hungry.

It took no time at all to get dressed and pack up their few things. Leo put on the same jeans he had worn yesterday and a clean gray tee shirt. A faded Red Sox baseball cap subdued his bedhead, which was worse than ever since he had taken a shower and fallen asleep with damp hair. America threw on a dark gray bodysuit with a thick flannel jacket that looked like a button-down shirt. The skintight athletic material hugged every one of her curves and left little to his overactive imagination.

Outside, the various hogans and RV hookups surrounded a central circle. Some of the guests milled around, packing bags or their cars. In the center, their host, Nahele, stood in front of a large grill with a flat cooktop, flipping what looked like a mixture of cut potatoes, sausage, and peppers. Beside the grill, a folding table held a large silver coffee dispenser, stacks of tortillas, and rolls of tinfoil. Leo's mouth was already watering, and America rubbed her flat stomach, though he doubted she realized she performed the gesture in anticipation of filling her belly.

"Morning, folks," Nahele greeted them with a friendly smile. "This batch of my famous southwestern hash is just about done cooking. Get yourself a wrap and I'll load it up."

"Breakfast smells incredible," America said.

"How was your evening?" Nahele asked as he spooned a portion of hash into America's waiting tortilla. "I missed you at the bonfire."

"We crashed, and I slept like a baby," she said. "You know, we own a place similar to this one back home in New England. We have a bunch of cabins and a converted barn which serves as the main meeting place. It's nice to feel a little bit of home here."

"Is that right? What's your place called?" Nahele asked while filling Leo's wrap. "I'll have to check it out next time I'm in the area."

"It's called The Foundry Retreat," Leo said. "What brings you out our way?"

"There's an annual tribal meeting up in Nova Scotia every year. I've gone a couple times."

Leo dug a business card from his wallet and handed it over. "We'd be happy to have you if you're ever our way."

"It seems like you are a long way from home. Where are you heading today?" Nahele asked as he scooped hash into another guest's tortilla.

"Colorado Springs," Leo said.

"But we're stopping at Four Corners first. I don't know the next time we'll be driving through the desert, so we might as well see what we can see." America's enthusiasm was showing, and Leo was happy she seemed less stressed than she had yesterday. It was a miracle what a good night's sleep and some delicious food could do for a person's attitude.

"The corner is about thirty minutes away," Nahele said. "But, if you have a few minutes before you go, I'd like to give you something. I was hoping you would come to the bonfire last night, but seeing as you're here now..."

Leo nodded. "We have a few minutes."

Leo cozied up beside America on a picnic table bench and downed his breakfast. "If this isn't world famous, it should be."

America nodded while she chewed her last bite. Nahele finished serving all the waiting guests and disappeared into the welcome cabin. Some of the fellow guests milled around the central campfire and smiled while exchanging greetings. One couple took their tinfoil-wrapped breakfast and stowed it in their oversized hiking backpacks. The middle-aged man and woman, with their extendable hiking sticks, headed east towards a rather tall mesa protruding from the otherwise flat surroundings.

"This place is pretty incredible," Leo said. "It's too bad we can't stay longer."

Nahele approached with a woman on his arm. She was small in stature, but her weathered face showed strength and kind dignity. Her long salt and pepper hair hung down over both shoulders in tidy plaited strands and a smile split her lips where white teeth shined in the morning light. She put her hands out to America but said nothing and inspected America's dark hair and bright eyes.

After it seemed America passed the old woman's test, the woman turned and took a leather saddle bag from Nahele. From the sack, she pulled out a kind of flat bread and unwrapped the cellophane. She broke the thin loaf in half and handed a piece to both Leo and America. "Nahele tells me you wed yesterday?"

America nodded and stood shoulder to shoulder with Leo.

"I would like to bestow a marriage blessing as a gift to you," she said.

"Thank you. We would be honored." Leo had been feeling uneasy about how the last twenty-four hours had gone, but this blessing, so generously gifted to them, could be the thing he and America needed to feel their marriage was official. "This is very kind of you. We came in last night and basically crashed. I don't even remember what we said to Nahele."

"Such a beautiful, young couple. But I sense turmoil in your spirits and hope this traditional blessing will provide you with peace. My name is Doba. What are your names?" she said.

"This is America and I'm Leopold."

"Leopold and America, you have lit a flame." She pantomimed a flame burning in the palms of her hands. "And the fire should be kindled. Your blaze represents love and, just like a fire, your love must be tended to. The new ember, sparked by your love, represents a new beginning, a new life. No longer one, as two, your flame will grow, just like your family will grow. You are meant to be united until old age, when the natural course of a flame extinguishes and returns you to the ground," Doba said, and added a word in her native language. "Eat of the bread and burn the rest in the fire pit as an offering to the earth."

They followed Doba's instructions, taking a bite and tossing the remaining bread to the fire. With this act, a serenity settled inside Leo, and he released the uneasy feelings he had about the unorthodox way their marriage began. If he desired to have a love as big as the one his parents shared, Doba's blessing was certainly helping things off in the right direction.

They said their goodbyes and thanks and walked without words to their waiting SUV. America beamed as they drove the short distance to Four Corners. Though Leo wasn't speeding, exactly, there wasn't any posted speed limit on the dirt road. He was sure he was traveling faster than he should have; anxious to get to their next stop. Nahele had been correct, and the drive took a little over thirty minutes.

Pulling up to the parking area on the southeast side of the square, they crossed the border between Arizona into New Mexico, and parked. One other car crawled up the dirt road behind them but parked on the adjacent side. America hopped down from the car first and kicked up a cloud of loose dust with her feet.

"I'm not used to this free-wheeling version of you. I'm normally the one pulling you from your comfort zone, and here you are..." Leo kissed the side of her head as they walked to the center of the monument. "Running enthusiastically into new experiences."

"Is this going to be a problem for you?" she chuckled.

"No. I like it, it's different. I don't even see you check your watch anymore."

"Well," America said and skipped to the junction of the four state's border lines and lay on the ground like a starfish. "I've never been in four places at once. If I can do this, I can do anything."

Leo could see her pink cheeks lighting up as the morning sun kissed her skin. She was the most beautiful bride he had ever seen. His bride. He was still unsure how he ended up with someone that was so clearly out of his league, that he shook his head quickly to make certain he wasn't fantasizing.

"Alright," he nudged her over with his toe. "My turn to be multi-spatial."

She scooted and they lay beside each other looking at the various flags flying over each quadrant. Colorado, Utah, Arizona, and New Mexico. Leo couldn't help but think of how uninhabitable the landscape was in this part of the country, and that people, for thousands of years, had found a way to live in harmony with the land despite the unforgiving conditions.

Time ticked by, and his eagerness to get home and begin his life with his new wife swelled in his heart. Leo stood and brushed the dirt from his pants and shirt. He pulled America off the ground and to her feet and helped her with the dirt covering her bottom. She didn't seem to mind his touch, but a blush warmed her face. Whether they were married this week or next, made no difference to him in the long run, he was just glad to have the stunning woman beside him.

They snapped a selfie together with the four pie pieces of the border visible behind them and headed back to the car. On the glass of the rear windshield, caked with fine dust, America used her finger to write the words *Colorado or Bust*.

CHAPTER 9

A maid of honor's duty wasn't something Carol had plans to shirk any time soon. In her whole life, no bride had ever offered her the opportunity until now. Her job, up until yesterday, had been mostly uneventful, but now she was on full duty. America and Leo wouldn't be home in Christmas Cove for days. It was up to her to keep plans moving forward, and she was overjoyed to do the work... with a little help.

Carol could have just called Edwin, but she convinced herself to march right up to the front door of the man's little lodge. She peered through an open window but there was no sign of Edwin. It was a mistake for her to think he would be around, and she doubted that he would even want to help her.

Seeing the folly in her ill-timed expression of wishful thinking, she turned and marched right back down the porch steps. The thick scent of fresh boiling hops perfumed the air as it floated across the front yard, and she fought the urge to seek out the source in the attached shed.

"Carol, is that you?" Edwin's voice sounded from inside the shed. "I'm around back. You need somethin'?"

Indecision held her in place for longer than she liked. Carol hated to admit it, but there was something about this vexing man that she had always been drawn to. Despite her thoughts about running back to her home on Main Street, she entered the shed instead.

"I can smell your witch's brew from down the road," she teased. "What is it this time, rat's bone and grass clippings?"

"You know very well I don't use rat in my batches. It's squirrel bones. And I expect you to show some respect to the dead next time you barge into my lair."

Carol laughed at how ridiculous he sounded when he played with her. But this is how they were. Years of bitterness had begun to melt away last winter but only exposed an awkward unsaid truth between them. Pride had kept them apart for a long time, and the silly teasing threatened to unbind her steely heart. Perhaps her biggest mistake after spending all these years as rivals was hoping somehow, they could become something else.

Carol came around a copper vessel positioned in the center of the shed and crossed her arms in front of her chest. Standing near Edwin, she watched him wield a large wooden paddle and stir the contents. "I was only kidding about the rat's bone. It smells divine. What is it really?"

"I'm trying a new recipe; figs and pecans. What do you think?" Edwin said.

"It could be interesting. When will it be ready to try?"

"Soon." Edwin removed the paddle and tapped the liquid off using the edge of the pot. "It's for the wedding. I wanted to surprise Leo. He's the only person around here that likes my brews."

"That's not true. I like smelling them. But you know I don't drink beer," Carol said and wafted the rising steam towards her nose. She took a long whiff. "Definitely figs in there. Do you think he'll like it?"

"I hope so. I'm making a large batch," Edwin chuckled. "Do

you know if they made it back alright? I didn't see lights on in his trailer last night."

"Does Leo know you spy on him like that?" Carol asked and walked around the space.

She couldn't recall the last time she had been in the shed. Or in Edwin's house for that matter. A work bench skirted the whole of the outer walls, leaving room in the center for the woodfired brewing equipment. Various containers, casks, and tools littered the workbench in what seemed like no particular order, though she was certain there was a method to his process. Being a military man, he knew the importance of structure, which was probably the reason he kept tabs on young Leo the way he did, and anyone else he cared for.

"I don't spy exactly. But he parked that dang thing across the yard where I can see it from my bedroom window. It's not my fault he hasn't moved it in… when did he move back here?"

"Has it been ten years now?" Carol tried to remember but honestly felt like Leo had always been around. People in town say that *she's* the glue the community needs, but Carol knew the real bonding force had been Leo for quite some time.

"Either way, I'm gonna miss seeing him come and go when he moves into that house with America next week."

"Oh, right." Carol snapped her fingers and set her eyes on Edwin's face. "That's why I'm here. America and Leo are road-tripping back from Vegas. She said there's a winter storm heading this way, and since all the flights got canceled, they decided to drive back home instead of waiting until Friday for a rescheduled flight."

"That's a long drive." Edwin plopped a solid wood lid on the pot and snuffed out the fire below. "When will they be back? In time for the wedding, I hope."

"About that. I spoke to America yesterday and she asked if we could help with all the last-minute details, since she's obviously not here. Plus, I thought it would be fun and figured you had nothing better to do with Leo being gone. Not to mention, Grant and Thandie have been holding things down at The Foundry for quite some time now, without much assistance. And the town is getting along just fine with all the new businesses and people moving into the area. And—"

"Carol. Carol!" he yelled and stopped her rambling. "Of course, I will help with whatever you… whatever they need. You don't need to convince me."

She shouldn't have been shocked, but she was. She had spent so many years being known as Scrooge McCarol and making the lives of her friends miserable, when in reality, it was she who was unhappy the whole time, that she still felt as though she must persuade everyone. But now, it was clear that all she need do was ask, and the people who cared for her would gladly lend a hand.

Edwin had taken her by the shoulders, though she hadn't realized when exactly. Her eyes followed the line of his arm towards his chest and up to his face. He was older now than he was the first time she had stood before him so closely. His weathered skin framed the same caring look he had given her all those years ago at the winter formal dance. She liked the way his eyes drank her in now the same way they had that dreadful night before her life was irrevocably changed.

But what was, couldn't be again, she hadn't let herself think of such possibilities, and wasn't about to start now. Carol backed away towards the shed's double doors. "Tomorrow, we have a menu tasting with Alfonso at one-thirty."

"Great. I'll already be at The Foundry. I'm helping Grant with a special project."

"You and your special projects. I— I'll see you then," Carol stuttered as Edwin closed the space between them, no doubt sensing what she was feeling. A tiny spark, a little ember of a life they both missed out on. She looked away and her body followed her out the door. "One-thirty. And don't be covered with dirt or grease," she yelled back at him.

"No promises!"

CHAPTER 10

With the Four Corners long gone in the rear view, the red desert had given way to the twists and turns of a mountain highway that followed the curve of the land and white foaming river rapids. The valley dipped sharply between steep cut cliff faces and the road turned to the north. Their destination for the night, Colorado Springs, was now only a few miles away. America had held on to Leo's hand for so long. The moisture and heat caused their skin to seem glued together at the center console and she was afraid to try and let go.

Leo looked at her briefly and smiled. His knee held the steering wheel steady, a necessary habit formed from driving his old red pickup truck. He combed his hair back from his eyes the way he did when he was deep in thought, and America had to know what he was thinking about.

"What's on your mind?" she asked, though she suspected it had to do with the night's sleeping arrangements again from the way his fingers flexed.

"I was just thinking about how lucky you are to have your very own mountain. Look, there it is." Leo pointed out the driver's window. "America's Mountain, Pikes Peak."

"Sounds like Pike's mountain, not mine," she joked.

To the west, America watched the sun take its final breath and dip behind the towering mountain peaks. Fingers of sunlight jutted through the splintered terrain and cut brilliant golden streaks through the darkening sky. Colorado had one of the most beautiful landscapes she had ever seen. The rolling hills and pine forests reminded her of New England, but the deep valleys and snow-frosted heights were a dazzling sight to behold. "It is beautiful, isn't it?"

"Yes, you are," Leo flattered.

A little cheesy, she thought, but she loved how he showered her with love. She thanked him with a kiss on his shoulder and kept her eyes trained on the scenery. The mountains, tall and broad, were a mere silhouette, but the city was coming to life with thousands of twinkling lights decorating the dimming horizon ahead. If she didn't know better, she would have thought it was Christmas time, not February. "Do you suppose it's the cold, clean air that makes the lights sparkle like that?"

"Probably. And I've never seen so many stars, and it's not even all the way dark outside yet." Leo leaned forward and gazed up through the front windshield.

"Eyes. Road," America reminded him, though he was right to want to see. "I have an idea. Why don't we grab something to eat and then find a place to snuggle under the stars."

"Sounds good to me."

"Burgers?" she asked.

"Sounds good to me," Leo chuckled.

"A man of few words," America said and opened the map app on her phone.

"A hungry man has no need for wasting energy on words," Leo explained with more words than were necessary to get his point across. At least she finally understood why he had been so quiet during the last hour of the trip. He was hungry.

America directed Leo to a burger place, and after a quick

internet search of the best places to stargaze in Colorado Springs, Leo headed to a park called The Garden of the Gods. Just off the interstate, he followed the road as it snaked around gigantic monuments and delicate spires. He found a small empty parking area situated near the base of what appeared to be a giant red platter stuck into the ground and balancing on its thin edge.

America looked up through the windshield. "Do you think it'll fall over?"

"Let's hope not until after we eat. Why don't you grab the food and meet me upstairs," Leo said and opened the back door.

"Upstairs?" she asked, not quite knowing what he was talking about.

America slipped her arms through her coat sleeves and zipped up her red puffer. Gathering dinner, which consisted of two cheeseburgers, fries, and a large Dr. Pepper, she met Leo at the front of the car. He sat with his legs crisscrossed and invited her up to join him on the hood. "Upstairs," she giggled.

The hood was still warm from the engine heat, though the air felt like tiny little ice knives cutting her exposed skin. Leo unrolled a large southwestern style blanket and draped it over their shoulders as they sat looking westward.

Pulling the soft fabric around her legs on the far side, she asked, "Where did you get this?"

"Nahele must have thrown it in the back before we left the hogans. Here," he passed her a small, folded notecard, "he left this note."

She opened the small card. "Leo and America. Congratulations on your marriage. I hope this blanket will keep you close on cold nights and hold you together when times are tough. Best wishes, Nahele and Doba." America tucked the note inside her coat pocket. "That's incredibly sweet. Why do you think they took such a liking to us?"

Leo unwrapped the brown parchment paper from around his burger and lapped up the melting cheese where it was dripping out of one side of the bun. "I think people just get a feeling about other people. Like I did when I met you. Or like you did when you met Carol. You just knew she was a nut waiting for someone to come crack that hardheaded shell of hers."

America laughed. "When you so sweetly told me to go and speak with her about decorating the town for Christmas and I had no idea what I was getting myself into. I think if you had told me what to expect I may have formed an opinion about her, a wrong one, and never tried to be her friend. So, I guess I know what you mean. As for you, I thought you might be an ax murderer when we first met."

"I'm glad you're over that."

"Who said I am?" She laughed.

"How do you know I'm not?" Leo gave a diabolical chortle back knowing how many true-crime podcasts America used to listen to. It was no surprise that her mind had gone there. *Just one more reason to love her*, he thought. "Remind me to send Nahele a thank you note once we get back home." Leo took another bite of his burger as the sky turned from a dull purple to a dark blue. "You're not eating?"

"I'm not hungry." America looked down at her wrapped burger, and her stomach growled loudly, causing them both to giggle. "I guess I'm hungrier than I thought."

Once their dinner was gone, and the hood of the car was nearly cooled off, the sky was filled with millions of little specks of light. Leo laid back and used the windshield as a headrest, while America snuggled into the crook of his arm. He was warm, though the air was not, and he smelled like bacon and cheddar. Through his coat, she listened to his steady breathing and strong heartbeat. Leo pulled the blanket over their bodies, and they took in the magical night sky.

To have and to hold... The words played in her mind in time with his heartbeat. *To have. To hold. To have. To hold.*

No matter how hard she had fought the reality that they were in fact married now, she had to admit that the air had changed between them the second they signed the papers in the Paris Hotel ballroom. It wasn't enough for America to know the truth, she wanted to show Leo, her husband, how much he meant to her. She took his hand and hugged it into her chest. The blanket was wrapped tightly around their bodies and giving them all the warmth that it could provide, but she snuggled closer anyway.

"Not the honeymoon you were imagining?" she said.

Leo flexed his arm around her, pulling her body closer to his, if that was even possible. Her cheeks heated and she knew it wasn't from the cozy blanket. "Better," he said and kissed the top of her head.

"Better? Than Italy?"

"Oh no, I didn't say that. We're still going to Italy next week. At first, I felt like marrying you was all wrong—"

"Hey," she nudged him.

"Not like that. I just had this picture in my head of what our marriage was going to look like. And accidentally getting hitched in Vegas was not what I had in mind with my Valentine's surprise." Leo squirmed and his chest muscles tensed as he offered an explanation as to why this trip was better than what he had imagined. "You know how perfect my parents' marriage was. I just keep thinking all the stuff that's being thrown our way... Is it a sign?"

America sat up and inspected his face for the truth. "So, you think that your parents' lives were perfect because they loved each other so much? I don't think that's how that works, Leo. I'm sure they had their fair share of hiccups. You just didn't notice, because despite any obstacles they faced, their love for each other got them through it all. And that's what you saw as their child. And that's all you're choosing to remember now as an adult."

"Like I only saw what I wanted to see?"

"Not exactly." She laid her head on his chest. "I just think it's not a good idea to compare our relationship to this idealized version of what you think your parents had. Because I can tell you right now, we can't compete with all that. Nor should we have to."

America was sensitive to the fact that Leo's mom and dad had each passed away only a few weeks apart. His mother died of a broken heart not long after his father's heart attack. Leo had told her that he longed for a love as big as theirs. One that was so big, only angels can carry it. That kind of pressure had weighed on her ever since and only increased after their engagement. But now, as they lay together, far from home, she wondered if their love was growing in big ways too.

"Look," she said, "a shooting star."

"I saw it too," Leo pointed to the area of the sky where the streak of light had been. "Quick, make a wish."

America squeezed her eyes shut and wished for Leo to kiss her. Not just any kiss. A kiss that would bind them together. A kiss that would say all the unsaid things in his heart. She opened her eyes, and the twinkling stars flooded her vision. She looked up at Leo to find his eyes still closed. A small twitch pulled his cheek up on one side, and she watched until he was finished with his rather long wish list.

"The reason I said that this trip was better than what I thought our honeymoon would be, was because I don't think we would have ever road-tripped like this otherwise. We spent our first night together as a married couple in the most beautiful desert landscape. Climbed mountain passes and forded streams today. I saw a herd of elk which by the way, are way bigger than I thought they were, and I ate dinner with the most incredible, gentle, understanding wife a man could hope for, under the stars in God's Garden. I made a wish upon a star, like something out of a dream, and I kissed the prettiest girl in the world."

The last part wasn't true, but the way his eyes smoldered with fire burned into her and let her know that he was about to make good on the last part of his particular wish.

Brushing her hair back behind her ear with his thumb, his hand came around her face. Leo supported himself on one elbow and half of his body hovered above her. His lips pressed against her exposed neck, just below her ear. Another caress landed beside the first. The night air froze the moisture from his lips like little crystalized tattoos dotting her flesh where he had just been. Tiny gooseflesh prickled up with anticipation across her body and she ached for him to soothe it.

His hand cradled her neck, and he tilted her head backwards slightly. A better angle for him to fit his mouth with hers. The kiss was everything she needed it to be. Pleasure heated her spine and chest as she succumbed to the delicious exhilaration of kissing her husband under the stars.

What was he thinking? What was she thinking? She couldn't put her thoughts together as his free hand explored her curves under the blanket. A moan escaped her throat, and he broke away only to crash against the spot where the sound had emanated from. She whispered his name and her body squirmed as she yearned for more; more of something she wasn't entirely knowledgeable about.

No matter what her body was screaming for her to do, she was out of time to find out where her limits might end. Gravel crunched under the weight of an approaching vehicle and the headlamps shone across their faces. A white pickup truck pulled alongside and parked. Breathlessly, Leo chuckled into America's neck at nearly being caught in a compromising position.

A flashlight beam blinded America and she put a palm up to block the worst of it. "Hey. Turn that thing off."

"This area is off limits after seven," a booming voice said from behind the light. "And it's seven-thirty."

America sat up and gathered the blanket to her chest. "Sorry, sir. I didn't realize," she said and slid off the hood. Her feet landed in the rough crushed stone on the side of the roadway. "We lost track of time. Thank you for reminding us."

"Kids these days," the man said, as he rolled up his window, in a tone that was meant to be under his breath but one she heard loud and clear.

Back in their own car, America and Leo giggled and exchanged little kisses and knowing looks all the way to the hotel at the highway entrance. She only hoped the place had a vacancy, and a cold shower.

CHAPTER 11

So much for that winter storm, Carol thought as she looked to the partly sunny skies above her. America and Leo had warned her of the incoming snow, though as she walked the mile or so from her house on Main Street down to The Foundry, she wondered if the forecast had changed.

Carol stepped along the newly built replica of a historic covered bridge; the kind New England is known for having. Though most of the covered bridges had long since fallen into disrepair, this one was solid steel and stone. Only the materials used made it appear much older than it was. She appreciated the effort in making The Foundry hold true to the area's nostalgia.

When Leo had first said that he was going to cobble together several of the old cabins and houses along the lake shore and create a retreat where people could come and relax, learn, and feel part of something, she had laughed him off. The idea was absurd. First, he was the mayor who saw the town fall to new lows and then he decided to be a hotel manager.

She had to give it to him though, as the black barn came into view, the risk had been worth taking. The resort was coming up on one year in operation, and other than the near catastrophic flooding that tried its best to wipe the place off the map late last spring, the resort was doing quite well. Leo and America had received an investment from an out-of-towner and were able to use the funds to make some timely improvements, like water mitigation.

Sunshine spilled through the glass exterior walls of the resort's main building and refracted off the crystal chandelier hanging just inside the vaulted structure. The luxurious sight was one of Carol's favorite renovations that Leo had undertaken at the property. The change that the abandoned lake-side property had undergone in the last year was unbelievable. Even though she had helped however she could during the renovation, the sheer scope of the project had been an ambitious endeavor that the whole town had gotten involved with.

And the guest response had been largely positive, seeing as how the place was always booked up. Today was no different. A dozen cars were parked in the recently paved lot beside the barn; Harbour House, they called it. This week's retreat guests were scheduled to check out on Friday, leaving room in the staff's schedule to organize Saturday's big wedding.

Inside, there was no sign of Edwin, who had said he would meet her there. Carol went to the *Cucina* where she hoped to find the chef and get the tasting moving along with or without Edwin's help. "Alfonso? Are you in here?" She poked her head inside the saloon-style kitchen doors, but the space was deserted.

The Harbour House was the main gathering space for the resort. A large, wide open great room where all the meals and many of the activities could be held. Saturday, the venue would be transformed into a magical garden for the wedding ceremony. America had been very vocal about the aesthetic she wanted. Pink and white would be everywhere.

Above Carol, the afternoon sun played in the crystal chandelier, sending rainbows dancing in all directions, and painting the walls with vibrant colors and geometric shapes. She could have sat there for hours just watching the way the space changed throughout the day, but alas, she had a job to do.

Carol peered through the lobby entrance for any sign of Edwin. "Where are you?" she said and plopped down in an oversized velvet chair by the two-story stone fireplace. Resigned to waiting on a man, or in this case, two men, she picked flaking red polish off her thumbnail. She knew better, it was a terrible habit, but had planned on redoing her manicure later in the week before the wedding.

That's when she heard the laughter of a man who was late. She stood and turned on her heel toward the back area where the sound echoed down the hallway. With a hand on her hip, which she hoped would forcefully project her displeasure at having had to wait, she eyed Edwin and the chef approaching from the offices. Edwin caught a glimpse and smirked.

"You're late," she said.

"Come now, Carol. You're the late one. We got started, oh I don't know, fifteen minutes ago or so?" he asked Alfonso.

"*Si*. Yes. We finish already, the tasting," Alfonso said in his broken Italian-English and chuckled at himself. "I kid you. Come and see what Alfonso has prepared."

Carol followed the chef to a table in the back, set up near the exercise room, but away from the other guest areas. The small, square table, likely pulled in from the dining room, had a white cloth and an empty vase sitting at the center. Alfonso reached to pull out her chair, but Edwin intercepted the gesture.

"Thank you, Pa," she said. Everyone called Edwin, Pa, though she always thought of him as Edwin first. Pa was the callsign he was given when he was in the army. Desert Storm had not been kind to him. He had left Christmas Cove as a young man and returned hardened and weathered, as though he had witnessed more during his time as a soldier than all the time before or since.

Alfonso excused himself, and Carol fidgeted with her skirt

under the table as they waited for him to return with the first course. Across from her, Edwin sat, his head tilted, and his eyes squinted at her. His hair was wet, like he'd just taken a shower before the meeting, and he smelled of pine and earth.

"You clean up nicely," she said.

"So do you," he said sweetly, though his comment only made her fidget more.

Why was she being so ridiculous? She had been around this man for more years than she could count. So why now, why did she feel like a girl on a first date? Before she had more time to think on it, Alfonso returned from the *cucina* with two plates in hand.

Placing them on the table, Alfonso beamed. His smile likely could not have been wider, and all his teeth shined. "I have first, *piccola* potato croquette. Lump crab cake with fresh fig and honey compote. A butter lettuce salad with local cranberries and Italian feta cheese. *Mangia.*"

"Well, I've not seen something this pretty in a long time. Looks too good to actually eat," Edwin said and cut a croquette in half. "What is a croquette anyhow?"

"I believe it's just a fancy fried potato. And you do know what a crab cake is, right? But I've never had fig and honey compote before." She looked Edwin in the eye and pointed her empty fork at him. "It's like a jam, in case you were about to ask."

"How do you know about all this stuff?" he asked as though he really had no clue.

Carol was reminded again of all the ways in which Edwin didn't really know her. Over the last year, as they finally put their rivalry away and began to spend more time together, they had begun to relearn things about one another. She had enjoyed getting to know him as he was now, and she wondered if he felt the same.

"I was in culinary school for a couple years," she admitted and stuffed her mouth with a bite of lettuce.

"Culinary school? How did I never know that?" he said, though she wondered if he should have his memory checked as she was sure he knew about her leaving town after high school.

She finished chewing while deciding how much she wanted to say but figured it wouldn't hurt for him to know her better. "That's right. Two years. You probably don't remember because you were stationed overseas, and I was trying to be anywhere but here."

Edwin laughed in his throat. "Forgive me, but I didn't even know you could cook anything."

"I suppose you never asked. And I... I never invited you over for a meal."

"I never knew you wanted to." Edwin chewed a bite of crab. "Gosh, Carol, you didn't even speak to me unless it was to complain about something or offer a snarky little remark when we passed on the street. That's why we called you Scrooge for so long."

Carol knew he was right but hearing him say it so plainly wasn't easy. She ate the rest of her food without a single additional comment, not to punish him, but she was deeply aware of just how much damage she had done with her words.

The silence was easily explained by how delicious the food was so far. It was the best she'd ever had, but even saying as much out loud, she feared she would go on to say something about some other topic that she would regret later. Getting older meant there wasn't much time left for second chances or second guessing, and she didn't plan on heaping more poor decisions onto her pile.

Alfonso returned with another set of dishes and expertly removed the emptied plates before setting the new ones down. "I see you liked very much, the first course. Now I have traditional rabbit stew, like the pilgrims ate." He giggled in the way foreigners do when there's something amusing about American culture, but his enthusiasm frightened Carol all the same. "With whipped mascarpone and shallots," he said and left them to eat.

"Now this is something I can sink my teeth into," Edwin said and slurped the stew from a wide spoon.

"I'm a little skeptical, to be honest. And I'm not sure America will like this," Carol said and stirred the ingredients around the bowl. "She's a city girl after all."

"Was."

"Excuse me?"

Edwin paused his spoon midair between the bowl and his mouth. "She *was* a city girl. Now she's a Cove girl. This stew is really good. You should try it."

Carol put a little bit of each ingredient on her spoon and brought the mix of green and orange vegetables and pinkish-colored meat up to her nose. She smelled the stew expecting something pungent or gamey. Instead, the scent of onions, sweet cheese, and rich spices felt more like a cozy hug by the fire than the rustic, back-woods trappings she had imagined. She slurped the gravy from the end of the spoon first and then poured the remaining ingredients onto her tongue. "It's really good," she had to admit.

Edwin raised a brow at her. "So, we should keep it on the menu?"

Carol nodded. "It's unexpected in the best way. Alfonso has really outdone himself this time."

Edwin scraped the last bite out of the bottom of the bowl. "It's really good. If I ever get married, I want this exact meal."

Carol was surprised he had ever thought about his wedding. She never wasted time, the way she knew other girls did, daydreaming about her big day. She had never been married and never planned on it. Hearing a grown man speak about his someday-wedding was as odd as the fact that she had only ever met one man that could have stolen her heart. And neither of them had ever married.

"Have you heard from them today?" Edwin asked.

"America said she would call when she could. But I'm assuming no news is a good thing," Carol said and set her spoon down. The stew was good, but she didn't want something so heavy just now. "You want mine?"

Edwin reached around the vase in the center of the table and retrieved the bowl. "Don't mind if I do."

She nodded and watched him dive in. "I just hope they get back in time for their own wedding, you know?"

It was his turn to nod, seeing how his mouth was full.

Alfonso clapped and came to the table. A wide grin pulled his chipmunk cheeks and exposed a thin ribbon of white teeth between his lips. "So? Tell Alfonso."

Edwin dabbed the gravy from his lips with a black napkin and smiled with his eyes. He looked like a happy man. "I really like the stew. And the fig jam was really nice."

"I thought it was all delightful. The crab was my favorite, and I think America will really love it all," Carol said and stood, her chair screeching on the floor. "I don't know how you did it, but you somehow combined the local ingredients with the personality of the couple. Bravo, Alfonso."

A blush splashed across his cheeks, and he looked down. Taking her hands in his, he kissed the back of both. "Much to do before Saturday." The man gathered the dirty dishes and made for the *cucina*, leaving Carol and Edwin alone again.

"I appreciate you doing this with me. It was…" she paused for too long, though she knew what she wanted to say, she debated saying that she enjoyed his company.

"I had a nice time too," Edwin said as though he read her mind. "Can I walk you out? Maybe give you a lift back into town?"

Despite her knee-jerk reaction to deny his request, she leaned into the moment, and leaned into the warm fuzzy feeling she had when he looked at her that way. "Alright. You can drive me home."

At that, he smiled and took her arm through the crook of his elbow.

"But no funny business," she added with a dramatized severity in her voice.

All she got in response was a wink and a smirk. Edwin was trouble, she was sure of it now.

CHAPTER 12

Out of frustration, Leo kicked the remnants of the blown-out back tire of the overpriced rental. *Who rents a Range Rover for a cross country trip?* he thought. He checked the location of the VIP roadside assistant that came with the hefty price tag, and he was only a few minutes out. There was one benefit of getting a flat in a big city; fast service and plenty of street lights.

As though he hadn't had enough weighing on him trying to deliver his precious cargo to the second wedding of her dreams, he now had a very real concern about them getting back to Christmas Cove in time at all. Although Leo typically let things roll off his shoulders, there was so much pressure he had put on himself to get back home as fast as possible. The more he tried making things perfect, the more fate seemed to laugh in his face. And now the shredded remnants of black rubber mocked his efforts to get them home.

The trip hadn't been bad exactly, just long. Last night, laying under the stars with America snuggled up against him, he had wished for a sign that all would be right. He wished that no matter how rocky or unconventional a start they had to their marriage, they would love each other for better or worse, the way his parents had. It was hard to argue with America's assurance that they would look back on this time with joy. But a dark hole of cynicism was doing its best to lie to him, and he feared that if one more thing went wrong, he would want to call the whole thing off.

Before he completely fell into self-despair, the tow truck, and another rental car pulled onto the shoulder as cars buzzed by on the freeway. In the light of the headlamps, he exchanged the keys with the tow truck driver. A representative from the rental company handed over the key to a replacement car.

"Your vehicle will be ready for pick up at seven. The address is in the app along with a voucher for dinner," the rental car rep explained. "If you have any issues, don't hesitate to reach out. My contact info is in the app too."

Leo shook the man's hand. "Are you sure we can't just take this car the rest of the way?"

"I'm afraid we don't have any vehicles available for out of region drop off."

"Figured I'd ask. Thank you for your quick response. We need to get back on the road tonight if we're gonna—"

The man chuckled without humor. "No, Mr. Thorpe, you misunderstand me. Your vehicle will be available by seven tomorrow morning, seeing how late it is. I apologize for the inconvenience."

"I guess that will have to be fine. Thanks again," Leo said, and watched the man climb into the front seat of the tow truck.

America had stayed inside the Range Rover where it was warm, while he handled his frustrations out in the cold by kicking every rock and piece of debris off of the highway shoulder. With an adjusted attitude, he opened her door and helped her down from the front seat. "Looks like we're staying in St. Louis tonight," Leo said. "I know it's not ideal, but we we're only planning to drive another hour tonight."

"This trip feels like the longest... I mean, it's been fun but—"

With one hand braced on the doorframe beside America's head, he leaned in and kissed the tip of her nose. "I know you're antsy to get home. So am I."

"Can't we just catch a flight? Surely there's something from here that can get us home sooner."

"I thought that too," Leo said and clicked his tongue against the back of his teeth while he considered the option to fly again. Numbers ran through his mind; time and expenses. "Even if we can book a flight, I don't know if we can afford to eat the extra cost. You know how much it costs for last minute flights."

"Let's look anyway," America said with a bright tone. "You never know."

Leo had already opened the browser on his phone while America finished her sentence. His eyes squinted as the results populated the screen, and he blinked thinking he misread the numerals. "Twenty-six hundred dollars?"

"Seriously? That's more than our flights to Italy. Are you joking?" America gave a nervous giggle.

"And it looks like the earliest flight out isn't until late tomorrow afternoon anyway." Leo shook his head. "I figured it would be more expensive, but not that much."

"It also means spending all morning tomorrow waiting around." America closed her eyes and let out an exasperated sigh; the trip clearly taking a toll on her optimism. "I think I'd rather just get back on the road in the morning. At least I'll feel like we're doing something."

"You sure?" Leo asked. Despite America's nod in the affirmative, Leo felt the need to justify the road trip one more time. Perhaps he needed to hear it himself as much as he felt America did too. "If we get to Buffalo by tomorrow evening, then we're only a few hours from the Cove. It'll be fun."

"Wait. Why can't we just take this new car now?"

"The person said that our contract is for delivery in Elizabethtown. There's a huge penalty otherwise," Lee said and patted his wallet through his blue jeans pocket. Leo hated how thinking of money had become a new, unfortunate hobby since opening The Foundry last year. "Sorry," he apologized. "I know there are other things to consider besides the cost."

"Don't feel bad about it," she said and moved around him towards the rear door. "Things are just tight right now, with the wedding and the expansion. We knew it would be."

"Yes, but we didn't plan on all this. What was a sweet little gesture surprising you in Vegas, has gone completely sideways." Leo paused and saw the corner of America's lip pull up and expose a sliver of white teeth. "Not everything," he said and winked.

"On that note, we might as well enjoy the city, if we're stuck here for the night." America kissed Leo on the cheek and reached into the back seat to grab her puffy garment bag. She stashed her suitcase and dress in the back seat of the rental replacement, a small four-door sedan. Leo held the door open for her and she paused, halfway in. "Plus, I've never been to St. Louis."

Leo closed the trunk and went around to the driver's side. With his forearms resting on the car's roof as America got in, he took a moment and blew some excess stress out of pursed lips.

"You coming?" America called out to him.

Leo ducked inside and fastened his seatbelt, smiling at the way America lit up and nodded her head like everything was going to be alright. "The guy gave us a voucher for dinner; feel like anything?"

"Italian," she said with a grin and tapped her fingers together in anticipation of a filling meal.

After a quick web search, Leo discovered the best Italian cuisine in town was in a historic neighborhood called The Hill. And the best restaurant to try was Charlie Gitto's. Thankfully, the eatery was only a couple blocks away from where the flat tire had occurred. On the way over, he spotted a few nice hotels right at the highway interchange.

Leo parked the new rental, a basic little Nissan, and led America inside. "Table for two please," he said to the hostess, a teenager with a long blonde ponytail who wore a white polo shirt with the restaurant's logo embroidered on the front. She walked away, presumably to take stock of the wait times. The place was packed, and Leo was unsure whether they would even get a table.

"We can find somewhere else to eat," America said.

Leo took her coat off and draped it over his arms. "It's fine. Everything is fine."

The hostess returned with a practiced smile splashed on her face. "It'll be thirty minutes, is that okay?"

"It's fine," America parroted Leo's sentiment.

Seeing their disappointment, the hostess shifted her weight. "You know what, you can eat at the bar, if you don't mind." She pointed across to a bar area trimmed out with rich dark wood and brass accents.

America nodded to Leo and the hostess led them to two empty seats. She handed them a menu in a sleek burgundy leather holder and placed two cocktail napkins on the glossy bar top in front of them. "Enjoy," she said.

America read the menu quietly to herself, though it looked like she was looking through the paper instead of at the printed words. Distress tensed her shoulders and pitched them forward. Her posture said more than any spoken words could.

Leo slid the menu from her fingers and placed it on the bar. "You're worried, aren't you?"

"I don't know. I think I'm just tired," she said and took a deep breath, blowing it out through tight lips. "I was so hungry a few minutes ago, and now I just don't know. I like to have a plan. I like knowing what to expect."

Leo hugged her. "I know this isn't how you imagined your week going. But I know everything will work out." He lied, he gave it a fifty-fifty chance at best that everything would work out, but he didn't want to add his own doubts to her own list of things to worry about. "I'm sure you'll feel better after eating something. And that's something you can plan on. What looks appetizing?"

Picking up his menu, the first thing on the list sounded good to him, "Do you want to split two things?"

America nodded and he was glad to see a genuine smile painted on her face.

He called the bartender over. "We're ready to order."

"What'll it be?" The man leaned in.

"We're gonna get the toasted ravioli. It says here that it's a local treat."

"That's right," he said. "What else?"

"I'll have the Fiore Borghese and a glass of wine. Whatever you think goes best," America said.

"And any drink for you?"

"Water," Leo said and turned his attention back to his beautiful wife. "I shouldn't drink tonight. We'll have to make up some time tomorrow if you still want to try to get all the way to Buffalo. We can't pick up the Rover until seven. It's going to be another really long day."

"I know," she said and swirled the white wine around in her oversized glass. "But I really want to be there for Carol's dress fitting scheduled for Wednesday afternoon. I told her I would try my best to get there. She's never been a maid of honor, and probably figured at her age, she never would get the opportunity. But I couldn't get married without her by my side."

"We owe her a lot. If it wasn't for her and Pa, I don't know if we'd be getting married."

"Got married," she reminded him. "But I know what you mean. Those two are quite the pair. It's such a shame what happened with her father when he split them up back in high school. Who knows? Maybe they'd be the ones getting married."

Leo chuckled at the idea, until it sank in. "You know, I've

never thought of it before, but there is something between them, isn't there?"

"You never noticed how Pa always goes out of his way to find reasons to be near her, even if the pretense is something they can battle over? Or the way she looks at his bum every time he walks away from her?" America giggled.

Leo snapped his fingers. "Or how he's always offering her rides even if he's not actually going that way? I don't know how I was so blind to it. I suppose that since I've known them, they were always just Pa and Carol, the town rivals. But maybe they've been more all along, and no one sees it."

"I did." America raised a brow as their food came out. Rich spices and tangy tomato-scented steam filled the air around them. "Let's dig in."

"Happy to. This looks incredible. Thanks for suggesting Italian, I think I needed comfort food."

"Thanks for finding this place. It's sort of reminds me of The Foundry."

Leo looked around at a the lavishly appointed space that wasn't overly fancy yet still inviting. The dark woodwork and leather furniture provided a cozy feel to the space, even the bulkhead hanging down from the ceiling around the bar provided a sense of privacy and relaxation. He made a note to incorporate more private eating nooks in the *cucina* whenever they made it back to Christmas Cove.

America smiled as she shoveled another bite of pasta into her mouth, and all seemed right again in Leo's world. He only hoped he could get America back to Christmas Cove on time, and unscathed.

CHAPTER 13

Morning came again. America rolled over to an empty bed and ran her hand along the still warm white sheets where Leo had slept. But wherever he was, he hadn't been gone for long. She craned her head off the pillow enough to see the low-lit digital clock on the far side of the dark hotel room. "Not even six," she said and buried her head under the covers. Her phone had other ideas about letting her sleep and buzzed. She supposed her day was beginning whether she was ready for it or not. Reaching to the bedside table, she turned the screen over. It was Leo.

"Oh, good. You're up," he said without waiting for her to greet him. "I need you to get dressed in something warm and meet me downstairs in fifteen minutes. I already grabbed all the bags but yours, so just bring it down with you."

"Is something the matter? I thought we couldn't get the car until seven." America rubbed sleep from her eyes.

"Nothing is wrong. But I'm up to something." His grin was evident in his tone. "See you in a few."

At least America had perfected the messy bun, red lipstick look. Getting dressed in a pair of black leggings and oversized white knit sweater, she threw on her coat and tossed the rest of her things in the small suitcase. She had exactly one clean outfit left, but the pencil skirt and red turtleneck wouldn't keep her very warm, nor was it ideal for sitting in a car all day. If all went well, they'd be in Buffalo by tonight and she could find somewhere to do a load of laundry.

America rolled her suitcase to the door and flipped on the lights for one more check of the room. She spotted her phone charger and skipped around to the space between the two queen size beds where it was plugged in, even though they had slept side by side in just one of the beds.

Leo had been incredibly patient with her. She had built up their perfect wedding night in her head, but her expectations had been utterly dashed by the surprise marriage. With everything feeling out of her control, she just didn't feel ready to give herself fully yet.

Outside, Leo waited in the little car parked underneath the lobby portico with a boyish grin on his face. He got out of the car and opened the trunk, waving her over. Her body hesitated to move out from the comforting warmth of the lobby air. The automatic doors slid open and the frigid mist pierced her face like millions of tiny razor blades. It was so cold, even the car exhaust was condensing into a great white plume behind the vehicle before dispersing in the breeze.

Running across the drive, she tossed her bag in the trunk and slid into the passenger seat all in one breath. "It's freezing. I guess this is the storm that canceled our flights?"

After closing his own door, Leo kissed her cheek and put the car into gear. "It looks like we missed the worst of it. I think we've been trailing behind the tail end this whole time. Should be hitting the Cove anytime now."

"Should we call Grant and Thandie and see if they need anything?" Grant and Thandie were the directors at The Foundry but had become close friends over the last several months since coming to town. She was just as concerned about their safety as she was about the business.

"There's nothing we can really do from here. I trust them to take care of whatever it is." Leo pulled onto the highway onramp and quickly brought the car up to speed. The bright streetlights created a faint halo in the fog and daylight was just beginning to turn the horizon a greenish-blue.

"Now that you got me out of bed so early, what are you up to? I have to know."

Leo used his fingers to mime zipping his mouth closed. But he couldn't keep himself from grinning ear to ear. Whatever he had planned, he seemed pleased with himself.

"That's how it's gonna be?" America said and crossed her arms for effect. "Okay, Leopold. I'll play along." She had no other choice it seemed. America watched as the high-rise buildings went from looking small through the fogged windows, to looming large overhead. In the skyscrapers' little square windows, lights flicked on as people were beginning their days. At one red light, a dump truck with flashing yellow lights on top of the cab sprayed out a deicer all over the roadway as it went by on the cross street. A man, bundled in an orange puffy coat and black and white striped scarf wrapped around his neck and face, rode a scooter past them on the sidewalk.

Once the traffic light turned green, Leo made a right, and America's eyes widened as she took in the scale of the Gateway Arch towering over the waking city. "It's so pretty." Lights shone skyward from the ground and illuminated the arch's outer silver skin. The gleaming surface stood out against the darker backdrop of dawn.

Leo parallel parked on the street and gathered a brown paper grocery bag from the back seat, filled with something she was dying to know about. "Come on," he said and led the way to a grassy knoll directly under the arch. From the bag, he pulled out the gifted blanket and laid it on the frost-covered ground. "This is what I was up to." Leo handed her a small cardboard box and a cup of something steamy and hot.

She lifted the box lid, and the scent of warm sugar and sweet jelly flooded her senses. "I love this surprise," America said and wasted no time in tearing off a piece of pastry.

Leo took the other half of America's donut. "I was thinking about what we talked about at dinner last night, and I think that accidentally getting married and road tripping for our honeymoon is just adding stress to a time that should be easier. I know you see it like we aren't even married yet. No official documentation seems to want to change your mind, but my heart knows." He placed a warm hand on her knee and his eyes were wide with affection. "You are my wife, and I promise you right now, before God as my witness, that I will love you until my last breath. America, I'm nothing without you." Leo took a sip of coffee.

She processed his words, which sounded a lot like vows, and guilt twisted in her gut that he even felt like he had to convince her in some way. The truth had been there since Saturday and there was nothing standing in her way but an expectation that she had placed too much importance on.

"Leo, I promise to love you every day of my life. I know we'll have hard times and good times, but I also know this world is better with you by my side. There's no one else I want to do hard things with than you. You are my everything, and I pledge to you my heart, my fidelity, and my devotion to our enduring love."

Leo wet his lips and his breath filled the space between them. She leaned in and kissed him on the mouth. Her lips warmed under his touch, and she pressed her tongue against his. Sparks traveled down the side of her neck and stirred the butterflies in her belly, replacing the guilt that had been present a moment earlier. Tears gathered in her waterline at the new, deeper connection she felt.

There was so much honesty in their words to one another and

even more in the kiss they shared. As the kiss ebbed, she cracked an eyelid open to find Leo's eye open too. He was looking to the side at something behind her and broke away licking her taste off his lips.

"This is what I was up to. Look."

Over her shoulder, an orange orb broke the line of the horizon to the southeast. Through the fog, the sun glowed and spread wide across her field of vision. She had seen sunrises before, but not like this one. The ripples on the surface of the Mississippi River glimmered in the brightening dawn like little heartbeats that matched the pulse of the awakening city.

Being coaxed out of bed before she was ready hadn't been the best way to start the day but seeing as how it had still been dark out at the time, the actual morning couldn't have been going any better. Saying their vows to each other under a giant arch was more of a wedding than one contrived of and carried out for the pleasure of others. This private moment would always be theirs to have and to hold.

Leo brushed a bit of hair behind her ear. "I know this hasn't been how you imagined your wedding or honeymoon going, but I want this sunrise to be a fresh beginning for us."

"I thought I needed the big ceremony and clinking champagne glasses to feel like our marriage is official, but I see now that I don't need any of that. All of the planning and stressing over every single detail wasn't for us at all. It was all for them. For our friends and family. I think all I needed was to properly commit myself to you out loud. No matter where that happened."

"Does this mean...?"

She rubbed the tip of her nose up and down against his in a way to confirm his question. Biting her lips between her teeth, she was unable to stop her cheeks from nearly bursting with joy. "I'm so happy to be your wife. Thank you for bringing me here this morning, and I'm sorry it took so long for me to finally feel it."

"It's ok. To me, it's not about the day, it's about the life we're building together. I've felt like you were mine since the first day I met you standing alone on the dock. I startled you and when you saw me, you weren't scared, you were irritated. I knew from then on that I had to be with this fearless beautiful woman. I'm honored that you chose me."

"I'll choose you every day," she said and touched her lips to his. "As nice as this breakfast is, I'd like to get back on the road now."

CHAPTER 14

Carol winced every time the slushy snow sprayed up the sides of Edwin's blue pickup truck leaving the windows covered with grimy, wet spots. Driving in bad weather had never been something she liked to do, usually opting to just stay indoors. Today, she had no other option. With America still not back in town, it was up to her to come through for the bride. She was just glad Edwin had offered to give her a ride to meet Thandie at the floral warehouse. One more splash through a pothole at the parking lot entrance later, Edwin pulled right up to the curb at the front of the large building.

"You need me to pick you up in a little while? I don't mind," he offered, while sporting a grin.

She felt bad having to let the man down. "Thandie is bringing me back, but I appreciate you looking out for me," Carol said and put her hand on the door handle. "You be careful heading back in this weather."

"You be careful too." Edwin got out of the truck and came around to Carol's side. He opened the door like a gentleman and helped her alight from the truck. "These roads are gonna be a mess before too long. So, if you need me to come back, just call me. Or text."

"You know how to text?"

"Turns out you *can* teach an old soldier new tricks. And with the new cell tower," he pointed to the top of the bluff where one had recently been installed, "we actually get pretty good service around here now."

Carol flicked a snowflake off of Edwin's brow as he steadied her using his hand to support her elbow longer than was necessary. "See you later."

No sooner had Edwin left the parking lot than Thandie ran out to greet her. "Come inside and get out of this weather," Thandie said and helped Carol take easy steps across the slick ground. "I thought I saw Pa's truck out here. You told him I was bringing you home, right?"

Carol nodded as they made their way inside. She unfurled the knit scarf from around her neck but left her gloves on, as it was nearly as cold inside the warehouse as it was outside in the building winter storm. Having never been to a place like this one before, she hadn't known what to wear, but it turned out to be immaterial in this case. Her heavy sweater would be just fine.

She supposed most people were like her and had never been to a floral supplier before. The warehouse was meant for businesses such as flower shops, and professional decorators to buy their items at wholesale prices. She was neither of those things, but The Foundry had an account there which allowed for this special occasion.

Since Thandie came on as director at the resort, she used her background as a botanist to bring an elegant flair to the weekly floral arrangements. Every cabin had a unique theme and the retreat itself offered a rotation of themes each week from art to wellness, and writing. Thandie was a magician at using the florals to convey the desired mood for the given week and was a true artist.

Now, standing in what was practically a refrigerator, sweet aromas bombarded her senses. Thousands of tightly packed bundles of flowers sat in rows arranged by color. The whitest whites gave way to creams and yellows. Harsh artificial colors, like neon blue and lime green, dotted the otherwise breathtaking array of saturated jewel tones and soft pastels.

"And you know what all of these types are?" Carol asked, overwhelmed by the choices. "How do you know what to pick?"

"Well, Miss Carol, that's why you're here," Thandie took her by the crook of her elbow. "You know America better than anyone else in town, save for Leo and her parents, so I need you to be her eyes and ears."

Carol nodded. She was happy to help out, but this should really have been America and her mother's experience to have together. With America somewhere in the middle of the country, and her parents on that last minute cruise that they won in a scratch off, it was now up to the B-team to pull the wedding together without the principal party. And Carol did love being in other people's business.

"Where do we start? I'm sure you have some kind of an idea."

Thandie nodded and directed them to a section of lavenders. "I like this one." She pulled a light purple rose bursting from the top of a dark green stem. Though it was beautiful, the choice surprised Carol.

She leaned in and sniffed the fragrant petals. "It's nice, but doesn't America want pink and white? Or red? It's her favorite color."

"Yep," Thandie grinned, and one brow raised like she was up to something. "Now watch this trick." Thandie walked the long narrow space between overflowing buckets and plucked one stem after another until she had a whole bouquet in her hand. She returned with a makeshift bouquet and presented it to Carol. "Look at this, what do you see?"

"I see ten different shades of red and pink."

"And the lavender? See how it acts like a soft neutral foundation, allowing the reds to shine through?" Thandie replaced the purple with white and Carol instantly caught on to the ruse. "Now what do you think?"

"The white is too stark of a difference. It looks… Cheap. Can I say that?" Carol grimaced at her own harsh criticism.

In an effort to comfort her, Thandie placed a hand on Carol's shoulder. "Absolutely. This is the feedback I need." Thandie did one more pass around the buckets of flowers and returned with her own bucket filled with stems. "Let's go to the office and play around with some options. Plus, it's a bit warmer in there."

At a round banquet table set up in the front offices, Thandie laid out the various flowers and filler foliage she had already selected before Carol's arrival. Carol's eyes went straight to the branches with sage green leaves and dark fruit. "Olives?"

Thandie took the branch and paired it with a branch covered in tiny white blossoms. In the center of the table, she placed the branches in a tall vase with a wide mouth. The blossoms seemed to drip off of the brown bark, and the sage green leaves had an organic natural feel that would complement the luxurious natural setting of The Foundry.

"So, I was thinking for centerpieces, we could do something like this—" Thandie asked but kept her eyes and attention on fiddling with the various greenery. Carol could see how seriously Thandie was taking this task and how much her face lit up at working the process.

"Can we add some pinks to the vase too?" Carol interrupted. "Sorry, I'm just so thrilled about being able to help with all this. I never got married, so this is the closest thing I can get to it."

"Well, what kind of flowers would you have?" Thandie asked and tried a couple different pink options.

"Sun flowers. Or anything yellow. Yellow is such a happy color, isn't it?" Carol pictured herself putting a golden flower in her hair the way she used to do when she was younger. She instinctively touched the side of her head where one would go and felt her wiry silver hair instead of the wavy, sun-kissed locks she remembered having once. "I'm too old for such imaginings."

"You're not that old, Carol."

"Old enough to know what's past is past," she said and handed Thandie a third pink option.

"None of these are working. How about I work on America's bouquet, and you can take a turn around the warehouse. Just grab whatever you think America will like best," Thandie said as she swirled the tips of a cotton candy colored carnation to open the petals more.

Back in the icebox, Carol headed straight for the pink section, and remembered what Thandie had shown her about how to complement the colors. A bright, almost retro pink flower stood out against the others. Its wide petals surrounded a coral center with little specks of yellow that looked like golden glitter. She plucked one stem and inventoried the other pink options.

As she pulled a pale ballet pink rose from a bucket, her phone rang. She dug the device out of her coat pocket and answered. "America, I'm so glad you called right now. I'm with Thandie at the flower place. Calling to check up on me?"

America chuckled. "Not at all. I have complete confidence in you. How's it going there?"

"It's snowing, just like you said it would. But the flowers are coming along nicely. As a matter of fact, I'm holding some spectacular looking pink flowers right now. That is what you wanted, right?"

"Pinks, reds, anything romantic and dreamy."

Carol looked through the partially fogged windows into the office where Thandie was plucking petals from a rose. The centerpiece definitely had a dreamy, romantic feel the way the blossoms hung from the delicate branches. "I think you'll love what Thandie is working on. She really has an eye for flowers."

"I'm happy to hear it's going well. We just stopped for lunch, and I thought it would be a good time to check in."

"Are you going to make it back for the dress fitting tomorrow?" Carol asked. She was nervous about going by herself and really wanted America to be there.

"That's the plan. We're in some little town in Ohio right now and I'm eating something called Chili Five-way. It's so good," America said, though it sounded like she was talking with her mouth full. "Anyway, the plan is to get to Buffalo tonight and come on home tomorrow."

"What's Chili Five-way?"

America giggled at the question. "I'm not entirely sure. It's spaghetti noodles with chili, cheese, onions, and beans, and I think it's my new favorite dish."

"You want me to add it to the reception menu?" Carol joked, but America's long pause before answering made her think that maybe she was actually considering it. "I can call Alfonso if you want me to."

"No, no. It's not really a dignified food to eat in a gown."

America's mention of the gown made Carol think about her dress appointment. "Spaghetti or not, I'm just glad you'll be back for the fitting. I was afraid I would have to ask Pa to tag along if you couldn't make it. How ridiculous would that be?" Carol giggled and picked up an orange lily, having moved down the row from the reds.

"He'd probably enjoy seeing you all dolled up."

Carol was sure America was correct. Edwin would love it, but the man would have his chance at the actual wedding, not before. "Let's hope it doesn't come to that," Carol said. "How do you feel about blue flowers?"

"I can't say I feel much at all," she said through a mouthful.

"Heard and understood, dear. One more thing before you get back on the road, when are your parents supposed to be back from their cruise? I couldn't remember whether it was today or tomorrow, and I was hoping to enlist Vivian's help."

"I think tomorrow. It's hard to keep track of time while living the asphalt life,"

"America, really? Asphalt life?" Leo chimed in though his voice sounded far away through the phone call.

"How's the weather there? I'm getting kinda worried about this storm. Have you thought about what you'll do if your parents can't get back in time? Do you think you'll postpone the ceremony?"

America choked and began coughing.

"Are you alright?" Carol asked and felt helpless.

"She's fine, Carol," Leo's voice came through the receiver louder this time. "Some water went down the wrong pipe is all."

America cleared her throat and when she spoke, it sounded more like a croaking frog than her normally smooth voice. "I appreciate you asking about it, but I don't think it'll come to that."

"You wouldn't want to hold off and wait for them?"

"Let's just cross that bridge later." America cleared her throat again. "As far as we're concerned, everything is a go. Thanks for all you're doing for us."

"I should be thanking you for including me along the way. I know you didn't have to, but you made me feel like I'm real family."

"You are my real family, Carol. We're gonna hop back in the car in a minute, and you have flowers to arrange."

America hung up the phone and her face drooped. "I feel so guilty lying to her. The truth will devastate her." America dropped her head onto Leo's shoulder. "If we don't tell them, we'll have to keep the whole thing a secret forever. I don't know if I can do that."

"I mean, it is a pretty good story. What would it hurt to just come clean? We can still have the party and celebrate with everyone," Leo said and tilted her chin up with the back of his fingers. "I know it was different before when you felt like we weren't really married yet, but now?"

"You're right, I didn't feel it before. But there's no denying the fact the we did get married on Valentine's Day in Las Vegas." She cringed as the words left her lips for the first time since it happened. "Having the wedding in a few days seems dishonest somehow."

"But what else can we do?" Leo said.

"I haven't figured it out yet." America twirled the spaghetti around her fork and took a final, giant bite. A rogue noodle slapped against her chin as she slurped it up. "I need to learn how to make this... correction," she pointed into Leo's chest, "you need to learn how to make this."

"Me?"

"Yes you. You know I don't cook. Plus, you set the bar pretty high when you made me the absolute most perfect eggs on the morning after we met."

Leo chuckled at the jogged memory. "I was just trying to get you out of the cabin faster so I could show you the Cove before the fog rolled in."

"So, nothing changes then."

"Pardon?"

"Like this morning. Your not-so-subtle 'meet me downstairs in fifteen' wake up call to get me moving quickly."

"What?" he said with his hands extended out as though he had no idea to what she was referring.

He looked completely adorable, and America had to wipe the innocent grin off his face with a kiss. She took one last swig of water from the straw and dabbed her lunch's remnants from her face. "Let's get going if we're going to beat the weather."

CHAPTER 15

Coming into Buffalo late Tuesday evening, the lake effect snow machine had cranked up ahead of schedule. America had traveled through Buffalo once, only waiting out a layover at the airport for a few hours, while Leo had spent time on the lake nearby as a child. Neither of them had visited in the winter. What had begun as a wintry wonderland with little puffs of snow gripping onto tree branches and flocking fence lines had turned into slick pavements and dangerous overpasses. America was just happy they had made it all the way through town before things turned even worse.

Leaving Ohio, they had a choice to take a more southerly route; a path that would have brought them very near New York but would have been hours out of the way. With her overactive optimism playing tricks on her, they had turned north towards home, by way of Buffalo, and hoped for the best.

Checking in at the motel, the clerk informed them that they were lucky because the highways were closing all around the metroplex. This part of the country was known for experiencing sudden and extreme snowfall totals, and America was surprised at seeing it pile up as quickly as it had overnight.

In the soft blue glow of morning, she sat by the window in their hotel room while Leo was off somewhere procuring breakfast—something sweet, she hoped. Her mouth watered at the thought of Leo's sugary lips pressing against hers, the way they had last night. America's hands crossed her chest, and she rubbed warmth into her arms, wishing she had grabbed a blanket from the bed to wrap around her body. As it was, her pajama shorts and button-down weren't enough to keep the cold, emanating from the window, from pricking at her skin.

She retrieved the white down covers and sat where she had been at the sill. Leo's scent filled her nose, and she closed her eyes as she let it fill her. She could almost hear the remnants of his soft moan as his hands had roamed her body under the covers last night. His soft skin ignited desire in her fingertips and stirred her need to explore all of him. He had enveloped her soul, and her heart threatened to burst from how she and Leo fit together.

After they shared vows under the St. Louis Arch, her reasons for withholding physical intimacy from Leo no longer seemed valid in her mind, nor heart. Her adoration for her husband swelled when she lay beneath him and wrapped in his arms. Although their delayed wedding night didn't happen the way she imagined—in a villa in the Italian countryside with soft linen drapes blowing softly inside the opening to a stone veranda—she couldn't have guessed how making love to Leo would leave her brimming with joy.

As though she conjured him with her thoughts, Leo burst through the door with his hands full. He used his elbow to throw the bolt, while a pleased grin left his eyes wide open. "You look cozy over there," he said and made his way past the outdated art-deco bed-set to the small honey oak table in the corner. As old as the motel was, it was clean... and their only choice last night.

"What did you get?" America asked as the heater unit positioned in the wall below the window kicked on and blew lukewarm air up her pajamas. She switched from sitting at the window to sitting on the end of the bed.

Leo sat beside her. "I got breakfast. It's not much, but I was able to find a place a block away that was still open." He handed her a to-go cup with a dark brown lid, and she could smell the earthy scent of black coffee. "I got you a lemon curd pastry and some red velvet donut holes for me. But we can share."

She would definitely want to share, but first she took a bite of the pastry and it practically melted in her mouth. The lemon was a refreshing addition to her delightful morning. "Thank you for this."

"Don't mistake my actions as being nice. It's self-preservation really," Leo laughed at what he was about to say, and the joke was already written on his face. "A hungry America is a dangerous America."

"I object!"

"I bet you do," Leo said and kissed her nose. "But you know it's true. Now eat."

With a mouth full, she asked the lingering question, "What are we going to do about all the snow? Maybe we should have waited in St. Louis for a flight."

"And miss out on that five-way chili?" Leo teased. "No way."

"Do you think the roads will open back up this morning?" America sipped her coffee and peered out the window at the curtain of falling snow.

"It's not good. The lady at the donut place said the weather can last for days like this. The good news is that the local roads are being plowed pretty well." Leo popped a donut hole and grinned while he chewed. "I even saw one of those road vacuums that sucks in the snow and then spits it into the back of a dump truck."

"Oh my gosh, you're such a little boy sometimes."

"Oh, come on! It was so cool."

She couldn't help but love how he saw the world around him. "What do they do with all the snow they collect? Melt it?"

"They probably just dump it somewhere. Who knows?" Obviously, his curiosity had its limits. Leo threw a donut hole into the air and caught it in his gaping mouth, smiling when the sweet glaze hit his tongue. "Speaking of melting water, I think we might be able to go see it."

"See what?"

"The falls," Leo said. "I know you've never been. So, since we're doing this whole *adventuring* thing, we should at least try and make it across town. And then after lunch, maybe the highway will reopen, and we can get out of here."

"I guess I should text Carol and let her know I'm not gonna make it to her dress fitting. She's doing so much for us, and I feel like I'm letting her down."

"I'm sure she understands, this weather is sort of out of our control," Leo said and gave a reassuring nod.

"You're right, and if we're here, I would love to see the falls. Let's check the roads before we leave, just in case." America opened the map app on her phone that showed traffic and road conditions. She nodded her head back and forth while the information loaded. One by one, the street layout materialized on the screen. Some showed up yellow or red, indicating slow or no moving traffic, but the green ones, mainly the local highways, stretched a path across clear through the heart of the city and all the way to Niagara. "Looks like we'll make it. Should we go ahead and pack up and hope for the best?"

"I talked to the front desk clerk, and he said we can keep the room for now. Plus, we have to come back through this direction on our way out of town." Leo chugged the rest of his coffee and shook his head from the caffeine rush. "I love this stuff. Doesn't matter if it's good or bad. I'll drink it any way it comes."

"Just like beer?"

"I do love a good pint."

America put her drink down on the small dining table and met Leo on the edge of the bed, dropping the blanket from her shoulders. "And I love you." She straddled his lap and placed her knees on either side of him. Her weight depressed the soft mattress, and she used her leverage to push him back onto the bed. A giggle vibrated in her throat as her hair draped around their faces. "We don't have to leave just yet."

Leo held tight to her waist, pulling her hips against his. She liked how it felt to fit her body to his. She tilted her head and swung her hair around to one side, letting light flood his features. A fire lit his eyes from deep within him. No longer encumbered by the misplaced expectations of finally sealing their union, she knew what he wanted, because she wanted it too.

Sitting up on her haunches, she checked the time at her wrist and unhooked the watch clasp. Throwing the timepiece to the bedside table, she began unbuttoning her red plaid pajama top one agonizingly slow button at a time. She was fairly certain her tease was having an effect on him as he squirmed, pinned beneath her weight.

It wasn't until later, when they were in the car on the way to the falls, that she realized she hadn't put her watch back on. Being in love, and snowed-in, worked to scramble her brain, or it forced her to forget that she had ever enjoyed worrying about time at all. If stressing was a sport, she was sure she would have a rack of gold medals to her name. As she looked at her naked wrist, she wondered if her sporting days were truly coming to an end. She rested a hand on Leo's right leg, and it hit her that she was no longer in charge of everything. She had a true partner to share life with.

With or without a watch, it was pretty clear that they weren't going to make it back to the Cove in time for Carol's dress fitting.

All she could do was try to enjoy the rest of the day. If it ended half as good as it had begun, she would be a satisfied woman. Outside, the whitewashed city creeped by the car's windows, and America decided to enjoy the view instead of calling Carol to let her down.

"You okay?" Leo asked. "You're more quiet than usual."

"I was thinking about missing Carol's dress appointment. I really thought we would be coming into the Cove right about now, not stuck in Buffalo. Not that it hasn't been great so far." She felt her cheeks burn from a rising blush. "I was also thinking about how our morning went and how much I liked when you—"

Leo grabbed her hand, halting her words, but the action caused the car to swerve. Even though he was driving slowly in the slick conditions, Leo should have had both hands on the steering wheel. America had other ideas and laced her fingers together with his, rubbing her thumb along the back of his hand.

She was truly married now, in all the ways that mattered. The papers had been signed, the vows uttered, and their love perfected. She caught her undeniable smile between her teeth. Looking at Leo, who glanced at her at the same moment, they both giggled. "Is it possible to die of happiness?" America said.

"I don't think so," he said, beaming. "But it makes me happy that you're so happy." He squeezed her hand.

They traded looks the rest of the way to the falls. Following the GPS directions, they creeped across a narrow bridge and followed the signs, heavy with icicles, to the car park. Whether from the cold or from the snow, she couldn't see anything from the parking lot. Bundling up, they got out of the car and followed the marked walkways. The route to the viewing deck consisted of a series of slick sidewalks and short sets of stairs. Deciding to brave the terrain, they took the off-road path and avoided the icy sidewalks altogether, preferring the added traction of the deeper snow instead. Her feet would be wet and frozen before too long, as her boots were really more a fashion statement than ones meant for arctic snowshoeing.

Besides the snow piling up around her, the snowflakes obscuring the scenery were some of the largest she had ever seen. Not like the stuff in movies that falls to the ground like delicate glitter, this snow was like millions of frosty meteors hurling towards her face. The visibility was near to nothing, and she would be surprised if she was able to see anything at all.

Leo helped her across the last section of icy pavement to the observation area that faced north. The best view of the falls was on the Canadian side, not the New York side, but this is what they had since they hadn't needed to pack passports for the trip to Las Vegas.

Desperate to see the falls, America leaned out over the railing and peered through the dense precipitation but had a hard time making anything out. "Why is it so quiet? Even small waterfalls make some noise."

"Maybe it's completely frozen this time of the year," Leo said. "Sorry, I thought that we'd be able to see something. I'm going to walk down and get a closer look." He tossed her a quarter that she nearly missed catching. "Use it in the giant binoculars."

"You mean my step stool with alien glasses sitting on top of a pole?" America joked. She always thought the sightseeing binoculars were a hideous eyesore that dotted the most beautiful landscapes and monuments around the country. Putting the quarter in the slot, the lens covers opened inside the contraption. Peering through, she panned around to the west where the water should be, but the glass seemed to be frosted over. The view was no better than the one she could get by squinting her eyes through the daylight.

Leo was out of view and America knew she wasn't alone. *This is how those true crime podcasts always start*, she thought and was irritated that her best friend Poppy had always forced their section of the office to listen to the disturbing things. Slowly, she turned her head while using the binoculars to shield her face and saw another couple approaching her spot. Hoping that the couple weren't national park serial killers, she opted to scoot down the railing so they could use the device if they wanted to.

"Howdy," the man said in a southern accent. "Cold day for sightseeing." America nodded, but they came closer. "Isn't it something?"

"What's that?" America said and her heartrate immediately responded to the sound of Leo coming back.

"It's empty," the man and Leo both said in stereo from each side of her.

"Empty!" America couldn't believe it. "Where, how? Do you mean frozen?"

"They rerouted the flow of the river to do a geological study of erosion. It's a once in a lifetime event seeing it dewatered," the man said with a very excited tone.

He might have thought it was a unique experience, but she couldn't see much of anything to know whether it was, or it wasn't historic. For all she knew, they were standing in an abandoned big-box store parking lot and not one of the world's natural wonders. "Thanks for the info, mister," America said and took Leo's arm. "Can we see anything from over there?"

"A little bit more than from here," he said. "I'll show you."

They walked along a U-shaped railing. and she could just make out the far edge of the famous falls. She'd seen thousands of photos before and had a reference point for what she was looking at. Across the river, the silhouettes of several multi-story buildings peeked through the snow, and red and blue neon signs shone between flakes. Below, a tree-covered cliff ended abruptly in a mass of broken gray stone.

"It looks so sad," America said and took her phone out. She snapped a bunch of photos, changing the filter with every couple captured in order to find one that could cut through the poor conditions. Being somewhat let down, she knew if she ever got a chance to come to Niagara for a story, she would jump at the opportunity. "Looks like all we're going to get today."

"You ready to get out of here?" Leo asked as he put an arm around her shoulders.

Her fingers were red from the cold, and he blew on them to warm her up. She didn't mind his lips being on her skin either. "More than ready."

CHAPTER 16

Carol stood half-undressed in the fitting room and inspected her aging flesh. Though her skin wasn't as tight or vibrant as it once had been, she had maintained her shape well over the years, and she hoped the dress would show off her figure nicely. The only opinion she was scared to know was Edwin's, who sat waiting out in the main salon. Once America had let her know that she wasn't going to be back in time, Carol asked him to drive her there. Using the snowfall as a pretense for bringing him along, the truth was, she didn't want to go alone.

"Everything ok in there?" he said, though the sound was muffled by the heavy black velvet curtain and his distance from the fitting room.

"Sure is." She grunted as she wiggled to get into the gown. "Everything alright out there?"

"You know me and dresses," Edwin said with a chuckle. "Now are you going to come out here and show me the fancy thing or what?"

"Hold your horses. I gotta get this zipped up first."

The consultant, a young woman in her early twenties who was probably more accustomed to helping girls with their prom dresses than an old lady wearing a maid of honor dress, held the back open and spread the fabric. "We'll shimmy it up together."

Carol wiggled her hips until the waistband was over her widest part. She yanked up the front of the bodice and slipped her arms through the thin straps. Supple cream-colored satin pleats draped over her hips and cascaded to the ground behind her. The dress hem was shorter in the front in order to make walking in it easier and the back dusted the floor. Matching pointy-toe pumps with a kitten heel made her look far taller than she really was, but she didn't mind looking a little more statuesque. After all, she would be standing at the front of the chapel beside America, and Carol wanted to look good in front of the whole town.

Looking at herself in the mirror as the woman zipped her up, Carol saw herself looking as nice as ever. Radiant and glowing, she looked like the girl she had been the night of the winter formal all those years ago. The only thing missing was a fur stole and a man to hold her tight. Her skin might have a few more wrinkles and her eyes had lost a bit of their brightness, but she was still a pretty good-looking woman in her own opinion.

"You ready?" the man of the moment asked.

She took one last look and hoped Edwin would see her the way she saw herself. With a fresh coat of lipstick on, she pinched her cheeks for a youthful flush. "Close your eyes," she said as butterflies swarmed in her belly. She fanned her neck with her hands and swallowed the nerves down.

"Are you sure you want to show the groom your dress before the big day?" The consultant asked while smoothing one additional wild pleat.

Carol about choked. "Oh no, he's not the groom," she said in a hushed tone. "I'm the maid of honor and he's the best man in our friends' wedding. The bride was supposed to be here with me today, but she couldn't make it."

"I'm so sorry, I just thought—"

"No. Nope. Not Edwin. He and I had a chance, but that ship has sailed, so they say."

"If you say so," she leaned in and whispered. "But you two are fooling nobody."

Carol puffed, knowing no matter how she tried to talk herself out of liking Edwin, it was obviously written all over her face. "Let's just go show him already." Carol flung herself and all her layers around, kicking the back of the dress out of her way, while the consultant pulled back the curtain.

Edwin stood at attention at the sight of her. His mouth fell slightly open with his bottom teeth visible. With each step that she took toward him, his eyes widened, and the corners of his mouth turned up. "Wow," Edwin muttered and cleared his throat. "You should definitely get that one."

She chuckled. "I already got this one. This is called a fitting, to make sure I don't need any final alterations."

"I don't think you do," he said. "It's very nice. And you look very nice in it."

Nice? Carol realized at that moment that she was hoping for a bigger reaction from him. She now understood the fear she was feeling moments earlier about showing him the dress. It wasn't really about the dress at all. She wanted him to see *her* in it. Surely, he could say something more than *nice*. Carol's hands went to her hips where the dress pulled her waist in. "Is that all?"

Edwin reached for her left hand, and she gave it willingly. He held it above her head and motioned for her to spin. "I need a better look at you. You know, to make sure the dress fits just right." When she came fully around, his lips were tight, and he shook his head.

"What is it? Something wrong with the back?" Carol looked over her shoulder to see what she could see of her backside.

"No." He stilled her. "I'm afraid you'll outshine the bride."

"Oh, stop it." Carol slapped a hand on Edwin's chest, and he caught it there. Her breath hitched and she swallowed the butterflies trying to escape. And just like that, she knew that ship hadn't sailed after all.

Edwin let her go and stood back. His eyes drank her in from her toes to her lips where his gaze lingered. His intensity screamed of admiration which caused Carol's heart, and throat, to constrict. This moment was far too reminiscent of their first date, their only date, that she hardly noticed the consultant pinning the hem and adjusting the dress's little straps.

"The hem here is slightly crooked. We can have this fixed in an hour if you don't mind waiting," the young woman said.

Carol nodded. "Anything else needing fixing, Edwin?" she asked though she had meant not just the gown, but their friendship, too. It was no secret that they had spent the better part of their adult lives on opposite sides of a divide. What most people didn't know was how responsible she was for their broken relationship.

As though he sensed her inner turmoil, he shook his head. "I think things are just as they should be."

Though his words were likely intended to reassure her of their friendship, his sentiment sounded more like a submission to the past; to the way things were. Their relationship had made a turn for the best last year, and moments ago, she was feeling emotions she had tucked away a long time ago. She considered whether he was correct. Perhaps, there was no use in revisiting their past, and things should just stay as they are now.

"We can grab some dinner down the street while we wait," Carol said, knowing they needed something to do other than sit and stare at each other while they waited.

"That will be just fine," the consultant said. "Let's get you out of this."

Carol returned to the fitting room and removed the stunning gown in silence. Edwin shuffled around the store as he waited for her to emerge. Every scuff of his heel against the floor reminded her of the ticking of a clock; reminding her that she had wasted so much time over the decades.

At dinner, Edwin didn't say much, though he was pleasant and did speak about the menu, how good the ale was, and how nice she had looked in the dress. Each averted gaze and uncomfortable smile said everything else. With every quiet minute, the distance between what she thought she wanted and what she assumed Edwin wanted, widened. She wanted Edwin, but was resigned to having him as a friend, if that's what he wanted too.

After dinner and picking up her altered dress, they drove the short trip back to the Cove. Edwin parked down the street from Carol's place, insisting on walking her to the door. He carried her garment bag over one arm, and she held onto his jacket at his elbow. Friends, or more than that, she was just glad they were no longer enemies.

The air was calm and Main Street was beautiful in the early evening. The town had decided after Christmas to leave the twinkle lights up all year. Hundreds of tiny bulbs stretched in rows between one side of the street to the other like a canopy of little stars.

Carol looked up between the lights at the tiny falling snowflakes. Despite her earlier judgment that things should stay the same between them, she wanted more and hoped her assumptions about what Edwin wanted were misplaced. There was one way to find out. She slid her hand down Edwin's arm until she found his fingers. To her surprise, he didn't pull his hand away. Instead, his warm fingers wrapped around hers and pressed into the back of her hand. It had been a lifetime ago when last she held his hand in that way and the intimate touch transported her back to a time when she wanted to spend her life with no one else.

"Dance with me?" she said and stopped Edwin in his tracks.

"Now?" His face was a mix of surprise and suspicion, like she had a trick up her coat sleeve. She gave a reassuring tilt of her head and he nodded. Edwin placed the garment bag over the seat back of a sidewalk bench and took her purse, placing it beside the dress. Wrapping his right arm around her waist, he rested his thumb along the dip of her spine. He took her right hand in his left in a practiced manner, as though he had been waiting a lifetime for this moment. With a grin and raised brow, he began rocking her back and forth to the sound of the snow falling around them.

Carol followed his expert lead with each step, and when he released her and threw her into a spin, her breath caught. She bit her bottom lip as he rolled her out and then back into his body. A giggle escaped her throat, and he kissed her cheek as people do when courting. The kiss, brief as it was, felt like a million dreams colliding at once.

Their bodies swayed to a quiet hum coming from Edwin, a tune she couldn't identify, but didn't want to break the sweet moment with questions. For a while, they were the only two people in the world. She wasn't sure how long they danced, but she knew her feet were cold. She let Edwin hold her close and warm her heart. Her head rested on his chest as he tucked their hands into the space between them. With every sidestep, her mind swam with the memories of the high school winter formal and wished so many things had been different.

A contented moan vibrated in his throat, and he rested his temple on the crown of her head. "Can I ask you something?" Edwin must have felt her tension; her regret.

Oh no, here it is. It was time for the explanation she hoped to never give. "Is this about—"

"Yes," he said without hesitation, as though he could read her mind somehow. "I have replayed that night in my mind for forty years; even went to war to try and escape the truth. But I have to know. What did I do wrong?"

Carol stopped their rocking motion and pulled back enough

to see his face. "You think you did something wrong? All these years? You thought it was you?" The realization broke her heart. She had never wanted to hurt him, then nor now.

"Wasn't it?" Edwin's brows pinched in confusion.

She shook her head, unable to speak. How could she have known that in her effort to protect him from her drunk father, that he would have internalized her actions this whole time? But it explained so much. The realization threatened to break her down more than she could bear. Grabbing her things off the bench, she made her way down the sidewalk toward her house.

"Carol. Wait. I don't understand."

She shook off his grasp on her shoulder. "I have never wanted to hurt you. But please know that you never did a thing wrong. You are a hero and a gentleman. Why do you think everyone loves you?" she said.

"Everyone?" he grinned, which broke her heart even more.

"I can't do this." Carol marched past him. "I appreciate your assistance with everything this week. America and Leo will be very grateful." She dug for her house key and fumbled the jingling chain as she hurried to get inside. There was a reason she never wanted to speak of what happened, and she had done a really good job keeping Edwin, and everyone else, at arm's length for a really long time. That was until America showed up and hammered little cracks in her hard exterior with all that Christmas spirit and cheer.

The lock clicked open. "Goodnight Pa," she said and closed the door before he saw her tears roll down her cheek.

Edwin knocked on the door, just centimeters from where her back pressed against the cold wood. "Carol. Let's talk about this. I…" his hand thumped against the door one last time. "Goodnight, Carol."

She heard his feet shuffle down the sidewalk outside, and she slid her back down the door until she sat on the floor. With exasperation escaping her through every goosebump, she kicked her shoes off and threw her scarf and bag across the foyer floor. Why couldn't she just tell him that her father had threatened anyone who would dare touch her. Outside the winter formal, they had danced in the snow and caught little flakes on their noses and lashes. She wanted to kiss him. She wanted him to hug her in tight and never let go.

But fathers have ideas about their little girls, and *drunk* fathers have dangerous ideas about the men their little girls fall for. By the time culinary school was over, her father had drunk himself to death and she finally moved home to the Cove hoping to see the man she still loved. But Edwin had gone to war and then came back a changed man. Distant. Which is where their relationship had stayed since.

Pride had been her biggest comfort until now, but now she saw it for what it was. She cried out. Not wanting to go back to how things were, but what was she supposed to do now that he had danced his way into a new possible future? Love him?

CHAPTER 17

After spending another night in Buffalo, Leo received word that the highways were finally going to open by mid-morning. Although they were officially late getting home, lazing in bed with his wife was exactly where he wished to stay forever. But important things, like driving home and having a second wedding still awaited. He reluctantly dragged America out of bed and to breakfast at the same donut shop he had visited the day before. This time, the coffee would be hotter and the donuts fresher.

"I'm excited to get home," America said as she shook the excess powdered sugar from her pastry onto a white plate. "As fun as this trip has been, and it has been pretty good, I never want to take a road trip again." She rubbed the side of her bum indicating there had been too many hours spent sitting in a car.

"Never?" Leo asked with batting eyes. "I've liked it very much. Especially the part last night."

"Don't be vulgar," she said with a wink, and the apples of her cheeks warmed. On the table next to her coffee mug, her phone buzzed, and the screen lit up. "It's my mom." America stood from the seat at the counter and walked to an empty booth near the windows where pink and red paper hearts left over from Valentine's Day still hung.

Her mom and dad crammed beside each other vying for camera space. "America. I tried to call you last night, but it wouldn't go through. Where are you?"

"We got snowed in yesterday, in Buffalo. Service has been spotty."

"Buffalo? What on earth are you doing there?" her mom said.

There was far more explaining America needed to do than she had the bandwidth for at the moment. "Our flights got canceled out of Vegas and the airline couldn't rebook us until Friday. So, we decided to drive."

"Was it a nice surprise? Seeing Leo?" Mom said with a shoulder shimmy.

"You knew?" America turned back towards Leo who gave a finger wave. "Of course, you knew. You probably helped set up the whole thing."

"Guilty," her dad said with a mischievous grin. "Cam did most of the work, but I helped too. I'm pretty romantic when I want to be."

"He is," her mom said and rubbed noses with her dad.

"I appreciate it, I do," America said though she felt like she was still trying to convince herself that the trip hadn't been an exercise in self-discovery and learning to operate outside a plan. "It was definitely an unexpected weekend." America felt it was safe enough to admit as much. "How was the cruise?"

"It was very nice, *mon*," her dad said with some kind of fake Jamaican accent. "There we were, all tan, and relaxed, ready to come home and see our beautiful daughter and that handsome husband-to-be of yours, but when we disembarked, we discovered that our flight was canceled."

"Wait a second, you're not back home yet either?" America asked. "There's a lot to do, and I can only ask Carol to help so much. I don't want her to think I'm taking advantage of her in any way. What are we going to do?"

"Don't fret, dear. Everything will happen when it's supposed to happen."

"Your mother's right," her dad chimed in from off the screen somewhere. "Take a deep breath for me."

America took an exaggerated breath and blew it out.

"One thing at a time. When will you be back to the Cove?" her mom asked.

"By tonight," America said. "And what about you?"

"Your father was able to book us a flight to Pittsburgh, that's as close as we could get since that winter storm has shut down half the country. I guess we're driving the rest of the way, just like you."

"We still have all day Friday to sort everything out. So, stop worrying and enjoy this little pre-wedding adventure with your soon-to-be-husband," Dad said, and guilt panged America's core. "I hope you're being safe."

"Dad!" America wanted to climb into a hole and die at her father having to tell her and Leo to be safe.

"He's talking about driving safely," Mom said with a little giggle and America realized she had jumped to the wrong conclusion. Mom whispered into the camera, "But you are being the other safe too, right?"

"MOM!" America covered her face with her free hand. "Are we really doing the whole birds-and-bees thing right now?" She wanted to get off this phone call as soon as possible.

Vivian shrugged with a grin the size of Pennsylvania across her face. "We're only a couple hours behind you but let me know if anything changes."

"Will do." America ended the call.

Returning to the counter from the most embarrassing conversation she could recall ever having, America tossed her phone to the surface. "I don't know how I'm gonna tell them the truth about all this. If we lie, how will my parents ever trust us again? It just doesn't seem right, but I don't know what else to do. All the guests are expecting a perfect wedding like we're the king and queen of the Cove or something."

Leo chuckled but sucked it in when he realized she wasn't being hyperbolic. "I don't think they see us like that. And how do you know what their expectation is? Did you ask them?"

"They strung up a banner across Main congratulating us!"

"True, they did do that, but I thought it was a sweet gesture," Leo said and looked down at his phone screen. "They just want us to be happy is all."

"Exactly like I said. Their hopes and dreams are riding on our perfect wedding ceremony." America shoved a bite of jelly donut in her mouth. "What do you keep looking at?" she said, though her words were muffled by delicious pastry.

"The baker texted."

"Why?" She drew out the word hoping he would stop her soon.

"There's an issue with the cake."

She finished chewing and washed down the powdered sugar with a sip of hot coffee so that he could hear her clearly. "What kind of issue?"

"There is none," Leo said and hid his face behind a steaming coffee mug.

"But you just said there was an issue." Using her fingers, she slowly lowered the rim below his mouth. "Do you mean there is none, as in no cake?"

He nodded. "Sorry, America. I was getting the whole story before freaking you out."

"I'm not freaking out," America spoke as calmly as possible, although inside, she was for sure freaking out. "What happened?"

"The storm knocked out the power and all the cakes thawed out. Then the freezer leaked caky juice all over and shorted out some of the equipment. Needless to say, there is no cake coming."

"Can we call other bakeries? What about Alfonso, he can whip something up. Right?" America relaxed into her chair, more like deflated into it and thought through possible options including making cupcakes herself. "I can do it. We have plenty of time when we get back. This is fine. Everything is fine."

"If that's what you want to do? Sure, I'll help."

She leaned in and kissed his cheek. "This day had better not get any worse."

"You better knock on some wood. That's playing with fire," Leo said and rubbed her shoulder. The gesture was nice, but not enough to fix her mood. "I'll make some calls before we leave the hotel. As much as I love a good cupcake, I'll see if we have other options, okay?"

"Thank you."

"You want anything to go?" he asked, and America shook her head. Leo handed his card to the waitress. "What did your mom have to say, anyway?"

"You're sweet for wanting to change the subject, but I'm afraid it's not going to help this time." America sipped her coffee. "Their flight got canceled too. But Mom did say that she helped you surprise me the other day. I know things have gotten a little out of control, but I want you to know it was a really magical night."

"It was, wasn't it?" Leo tapped the corner of his wallet on the counter and sipped his coffee. "Are they going to miss the wedding?"

"They caught a flight to Pittsburgh and are driving from there. We'll probably get into town about the same time. Mom said not to worry, that we have all day tomorrow to pull everything together."

"For our fake wedding?"

"Yes! For a fake wedding. Now can we go before anything else bad happens?"

"Knock on that wood," Leo suggested again, though he meant it as a joke, she heeded his warning. With a balled-up fist and gritted teeth, she tapped her knuckles on the wooden counter three times.

"Happy?"

"Delighted," Leo said and took his card back from the waitress. "Thanks."

She leaned across the counter. "Your card was declined. I'm sorry, sir. Do you have another form of payment?"

Leo looked at America and rolled his eyes. "I guess our luck just ran out," he said and tucked his card away.

America took a twenty-dollar bill from her wallet and handed it to the waitress. "Keep the change." She turned to Leo. "If there's just one more thing that goes wrong..." she said as a warning while Leo held the exit door open for her.

CHAPTER 18

If stressing was America's sport, Leo's was walking things off, though he also enjoyed kicking rocks from time to time. Today had turned out to be the perfect day for a stroll to allow his irritation to subside. The motel was merely a block and a half away from the diner and, in addition to cooling down his nerves, walking the distance allowed Leo to stretch his legs before getting back into the car for a final day.

Dense snow and half-melted slush squished beneath their sneakers as they shuffled along the sidewalk. Steadying America with a firm grip on her gloved hand, Leo also hoped to keep her from checking her smartwatch for the hundredth time. It was clear the morning's bad news had flustered his bride, and there was little else he could do while she worked out her deep moral conflict.

Feeling helpless tore at his heart. He wanted only one thing right now. Ensuring America's happiness had become his whole objective and he felt like he was failing. There was no denying that he wanted a grand love of his own, but the more obstacles they encountered, the more he had to fight the little voice in his mind that he was sure was lying to him. He reminded himself that one rough day alone doesn't tell the whole story.

As they came around the street corner where a plow had shoved a pile of snow as big as small car up over the curb, Leo saw the culmination of all of his fears. He tugged America's hand and spun her to face him, not wishing her to see what he had just seen.

"What is it?" she said with a smile that dissolved as she read his expression. "Leo?"

"I'm going to tell you something, and I don't want you to be upset." Leo focused his eyes only on hers. "Do you love me and trust that everything is going to be okay?" This was his moment to prove to them both what sort of husband he was going to be. Was he going to panic and overreact to every bump in the road, or would he be a calm steady presence with clarity of mind to bring them through fire together?

America winced. "You're scaring me, Leo. Of course, I love you. What's all this about?"

He hated having to tell her what she was about to see for herself. His face hurt, he cringed so hard, and he pointed towards where their car was parked outside the motel. America turned her body first. Her eyes were the last thing to go. Her shoulders raised and then slumped as she took a deep breath. With a single nod of her head, she walked forward without uttering a word.

All their luggage had been tossed out of the car and lay in the filthy black slush where the road met the curb. His overnight bag was half submerged. The thin garment bag that held America's wedding gown was draped over her suitcase with the bottom end hanging into the grimy gutter. From their distance down the block, he could see how the satin fabric had soaked up the gray water to about halfway up the bag. The scene only worsened as his eyes shifted to the car itself. The rear window of the Rover had been shattered open and pebbles of tinted glass stuck out from the piles of snow.

"America," he said and reached for her as they approached.

With determined steps, she marched to the luggage, unabated by his grasp. With a skip, she kicked the suitcase over and took the dress, slamming it against the ground. Grunting expletives under her breath, she let out all the frustration that had no doubt been boiling up since last Saturday.

He reached for her again, but the scene was reminiscent of a badger attack. "America, stop it." She avoided his hand again and kicked the suitcase harder this time. "America. Stop. This isn't helping anything."

"Don't tell me I can't throw a fit!" she growled. "I think I have earned the right to be angry. I'm tired of this trip from hell. I'm tired of being in the car. I'm tired of sleeping in terrible beds. I'm tired of lying about being married already. I'm tired…" Her rant turned to sobs, and she collapsed onto the ground.

Although he reached for her, he wasn't quick enough to save her from sitting down in the snow. Her coat barely hugged her bottom enough to keep her butt out of the wetness. Leo knelt beside her and pulled her face to his shoulder as she cried. He ran his fingers through her soft hair and devised a plan to make it all better. If not all of it, his mission was to fix whatever he could.

But he had no idea what to do next. His bride was breaking under the stress of the week. She had warned him that if one more thing went wrong, she was gonna lose it. Having her belongings—her wedding dress—thrown out on the curb most definitely qualified as one more thing.

While holding her against him, Leo pulled out his phone and looked up the number for the local police department so he could report the break-in. A pop-up blanked the screen and read 'Unusual credit card activity reported. Your account has temporarily been frozen'. *Duh*, he thought, and his neck heated with anger. When the alert cleared, he remembered the VIP car rental app, and figured their representative should be able to sort this out.

America's sobs eased and she wiped her face with the back of her glove. "What are we going to do?"

"Get a new car and go home," he said. "Nothing's going to happen if we stay here."

America stood and picked up the suitcase from where she had kicked it into a pile of snow. She righted the bag onto its wheels while Leo retrieved his weekender from the gutter. Half his belongings had been rifled through and his toiletry bag spilled out in the middle of the road. While he gathered his loose items, America lifted the dress bag. When he came back to the rear of the vehicle, she had hooked it onto the roof rail and an oily dark liquid ran out from the seam at the bottom like moldy pond water.

"That doesn't look promising," he stated the obvious to which America rolled her eyes.

She pulled the zipper down and exposed the delicate white fabric at the top. The bodice didn't look as bad as the bag did, but as her hand traveled downward, the dress turned from white to gray and a line of brown muck demarcated the dry from the moist fibers.

"Nope. I'm done. I'm not going anywhere." America unhooked the hanger and dropped the dress bag back onto the slush-covered sidewalk and walked away.

"America," he said and acted with speed to grab the bags and the dress. Using the fob, he triggered the back liftgate to open. He tossed their soaked belongings in with the broken glass. Closing the hatch, he slapped himself in the forehead at having gone through the process of opening and closing an already broken-into back hatch. He locked the doors nevertheless and ran full speed in her direction. "America. Wait up," he hollered. Even if someone did see their belongings, it's doubtful anyone would steal such a disgusting mess after so much as a single look. "Where are you going?"

"I'm done, Leo. With all of this," she said and turned the next corner past the motel. "You want to know what marriage is like? It's seeing someone hit their breaking point and letting it happen anyway."

"You think I let this happen?" Leo said as he matched her cadence.

"If you hadn't come to Vegas, none of this would have happened."

"What's that supposed to mean?" he asked as all of his fears about not having a model love like his parents had had, crashed against his heart all at once.

"All I mean is that you shouldn't have come. I would have finished my assignment, flown home, and finished with all the wedding stuff just like I had planned to." America stomped along with the last couple words spoken.

Like a dagger, her sentiment twisted inside Leo. Everything was falling apart around them, around her. "You forget one thing; your flight would have still been canceled. You can't plan around God."

She stopped at that remark. "You're right, and now he's punishing us."

"What are you talking about? That makes absolutely no sense."

"It's the only thing that can explain how chaotic this week has been." America threw her hands up. "I can't do this right now," she said and ran ahead.

Leo stood there. "That's not how any of that works, America," he yelled out and shook his head at what had come out of her mouth. Did she really wish the whole thing hadn't happened? The most romantic night on the town in Vegas, nor the accidental wedding could compare with receiving a native blessing, or watching shooting stars in God's Garden, or saying their vows under the biggest wedding arch on earth. The best part was when he got to make love to his gorgeous bride for the first time. This accidental road trip was one of the best times of his life and it hurt that she didn't see it the same way.

With as sideways as things were, there was only one thing left to do; call in reinforcements.

Leo took his phone out and texted Vivian, America's mother, and hoped she was getting service wherever they were.

> SOS.

...

> America needs you ASAP.

What happened?

> Long story, but she's refusing to get back in the car and go home.

Where are you?

> Buffalo still

Hold tight. We can be there in a couple hours. Anything I should know?

> We accidentally got married in Vegas. She's wracked with guilt over lying to everyone, and now everything is going wrong. Dress destroyed. Credit card declined. Come quick.

CHAPTER 19

Carol had never wanted to have a housekeeper more than she did now following a long sleepless night. Instead of rest, she forced herself to deal with her emotional baggage in the only way she knew how; by cleaning out every inch of her home. However, no amount of sparkling and dust free surfaces made her feel better.

Maybe she had been wrong, all those years ago, for how she had reacted to her father's threats. Maybe she could have told Edwin the truth. And maybe she could have saved herself from alienating all the people in her life who ever wanted to care about her, instead of throwing up walls wherever she could. Over the years, she had been very good at cramming it away for a long time, something she prided herself on, but now that same pride was causing her grief and pain.

Needing a bolt of energy, she put the kettle on and ignited the gas stove below. While the water boiled, she sat at the little kitchen table where a scattered pile of photographs lay. Images of her youth stared back at her like ghosts through time. After high school, she had run away and never planned on coming back, nor did she want to remember the life she left behind. No matter how hard she tried to move on, there was this place, this Cove, and that man who held a piece of her heart, calling to her.

Picking up a polaroid from the dispersed stack, her past laughed at her. In the image, she stood beside a young Edwin, shoulder to shoulder in their formal wear, and in the background, a skulking father with a bottle of something dangling from his fingertips. Carol had been so blind to just how bad things really were back then, until the night of the winter formal.

She closed her eyes and imagined how that night should have gone. Dancing in the snow, with the man she was falling in love with. A kiss. A sweet embrace. A possible future where she and Edwin could have been happy. *But dreams don't usually come true*, she thought and tossed the photo back to the table as the kettle whistled.

She turned the flame off, and poured the hot water into a little teacup. While the tea steeped, she gathered the photos and shoved them back in the old shoebox. She rubbed her neck, sore from using the vacuum and mop all night. Carol didn't need a stroll down memory lane; she really needed one of those spa days, only she didn't want to be alone with her thoughts any longer.

Just as she finished her thought, the house phone rang. She only hoped it wasn't Pa. "Hello?"

"Carol. I'm so glad you're home." Carol was relieved to hear America's voice coming through the receiver. "I tried your cell but—"

"This storm. It's been a mess. Are you almost home? Please tell me you are."

"Why? What's the matter?" America said.

"Oh, nothing with the wedding. We have all that under control just like you planned. It's just—I could really use a friend," Carol said and stirred the darkening liquid in her painted teacup.

"You sound… tired. Or sad?" America said, and of course, she could hear it in Carol's voice. "What's happened?"

"Do you have time to talk? I'd rather just speak when you get home. I'm sure Leo doesn't want to hear all about my problems."

"He's not here," America said, staccato.

"Where is he? Wait, where are you?" Carol couldn't think of a good reason why they would be apart, unless they had stopped for gas or something along the way.

"I am at a diner. In Buffalo. I don't know where Leo is, and I don't care."

"America Greene, maybe it's you who needs to talk to a friend," Carol said and suddenly felt like her problems weren't as time sensitive as America's seemed to be. "This is why you called?"

"I told him I wished this whole marriage thing hadn't happened at all. Everything is a mess. More than you know."

"What do you mean?" Carol sat at the table, moving the teabag back and forth in her cup, "the whole marriage thing? Nothing has happened yet."

"First, he surprises me in Vegas, for no good reason—"

"He had a decent reason—"

"Fine. But then our flights home got canceled. And the bakery canceled. Leo's credit card got stolen or something. Our car got broken into and all of my things were thrown in the slush, including my dress. Not that I need it anymore."

"America that sounds awf—"

"Oh, and my parents' flight got canceled too. They're somewhere, who knows. And with this storm coming in, I bet other people won't be able to make it to the wedding either. The whole thing is ruined…"

America finally took a breath and Carol was able to get a word in, though she hadn't followed everything America said. "And you feel like calling the whole thing off?"

America answered in the form of a sound in her throat.

"So, why aren't you on your way home? We can't do much with us being here, and you being there."

"I just want to go back to Friday and start this whole week over," America said with a deflated tone.

"Believe me when I tell you, that's never going to happen." Carol was speaking now from a place of experience. "You can never redo your life, nor do you really want to. Listen, I'm not sure how you got where you are right now, but all you can do is decide to take the next good step. You don't want to say something or do something that you can never turn back from."

America was silent on the other end of the line, and Carol processed her own advice in the absence of words. America was certainly having a bad day, and was certainly overreacting, but hadn't Carol also overreacted to Edwin wanting to know the truth last night?

Hadn't she used her father's alcoholism as an excuse to not get close to anyone? The only person she hurt in the long run wasn't her father, long in the grave, but herself. And due to her actions, Edwin had suffered as she hid her heart from him. In truth, she had hurt everyone she cared about. Now, even if she told him the whole truth, could he forgive her?

Edwin had wanted her to open up. He had practically begged her to. And she ran. Fear had played another trick on her, and she wasn't about to let the same thing happen to someone she loved.

"America, you still there?" she asked, even though America's little sobs could be heard through the phone. "I need to tell you a story, and maybe, just maybe it will help give you some perspective."

"Okay," she barely said.

"You know about Pa and me attending the winter formal back in high school, and that our moment was cut short, but that's not even the half of it. I was in love with Edwin. I knew it for sure by the end of the dance, and I wanted to tell him. We went outside to get some fresh air, and it started snowing. When I nearly slipped, Edwin caught me before I hit the ground and possibly ruined my dress. We were about to share our first kiss when my father's station wagon ripped round the side of the gym where I was wrapped in Edwin's arms."

"I know all of this, Carol."

"Bear with me." Carol said more irritated than she meant, "Sorry. My fuse is a little short from not sleeping last night."

"What was last night?" America asked.

"I'll get there, but I'll skip the forty years in between," she said, and America chuckled through the line which was a good sign that Carol's story was already helping her. "My father was a drunk. And that night, I knew it was trouble. He had already threatened Edwin, or anyone else who would touch me. So, when I saw him coming, I stood up and kicked Pa right in the shin so hard that he fell to the ground. I'm sure my father saw the whole thing and he actually acted concerned for me once I got in his car."

Carol cleared the emotion from her throat and took another sip of her tea. "I was too embarrassed to come clean to Edwin after that and honestly thought I wouldn't see him after graduation. I left town, and he joined the army. That was that, as they say."

"Only, it wasn't. Was it?"

"Do you know I've spent decades pretending to hate the only man I've ever loved. And over what? A teenager's misunderstanding of the world. My shame at who I was, and my fear about becoming like my father and hurting those around me led me to a place where I did exactly that, only a different way. Don't make the same mistake."

"But you have no idea—"

"It doesn't matter. Whatever happened between you and Leo doesn't define your future as long as you don't allow it to. You love him, right?"

"You know I do."

"Does he know that?" Carol said and placed her hand on the shoebox filled with her past.

"I don't know. Not after what I said to him this morning." America took a loud raspy breath.

"Tell him. And then get your butts back here so we can have that party!"

"And what are you going to do about Pa?"

Carol thought about what she would tell someone else in her shoes. She would say to lean into the truth. "It's not as if I can make things worse with him, is it?"

"Probably not."

"Then I think it's time he knows the whole story. Then I can stop making decisions for him and let him choose what kind of relationship, if any, we will have."

"I suppose we both have some apologies to take care of, don't we?"

"Talk to you soon. And good luck," Carol said and hung the phone on the hook. Knowing what she had to do, and actually wrestling up enough courage to do it were entirely two different things. She threw back the rest of her tea as though it was a shot of something harder and placed the teacup back on the table with a newfound determination.

Her life no longer belonged to the memory of someone who never did anything to deserve her. It didn't matter that she was in her fifties, there was so much life left in front of her, if she could just get out of her own way first.

CHAPTER 20

Not that she was hiding exactly, but America had hoped for a little more time to cool down before having to face Leo. An apology was owed to him for the things she had said when it had felt like the world was out to get them. With a cooler head, and dose of reality that sobered her up, she knew what she had to do.

As Leo pushed the door open and came into the diner, a little bell jingled and announced his arrival. He brushed his wet boots off on the doormat and combed his fingers through his golden hair. He took a deep breath and scanned the seating area.

Standing, America waited for him to walk excruciatingly slowly toward her. She opened her mouth to speak, but nothing came out.

"Hi. Can I sit?" he said. Leo's normally rosy complexion was pale, and his eyes were red like he had recently cried. If she wasn't feeling bad enough already, seeing him so low was a pain unlike any other.

"Leo..." America reached for him, and he shrugged away. "Okay," she said and threw her hands towards her shoulders. "I deserve that."

They sat across from each other and the same waitress who served them breakfast came to their booth. "Back already?"

"Our car was broken into," Leo said.

"Rough morning. You look like you could use some coffee. I'll be right back."

In the waiting silence, there was no eye contact between them. Every time America looked at Leo, his eyes were down, staring at his phone screen. When she turned her head, she caught him glancing up at her in the reflection of the frosted exterior window between the paper hearts stuck there.

The waitress, with a tray in hand, placed two napkins on the speckled plastic laminate tabletop, followed by two mismatched mugs, a trivet in the center, and a whole pot of coffee in the space between them. "It's on the house," she said.

"Thank you," America said, and poured some coffee into Leo's red mug.

The warm drink mellowed them both out, and after trading a few looks, there was no hiding their attraction for one another. Scowls turned to smiles, and when Leo winked at her over the rim of his mug, she couldn't help but crack. "Leo, I—"

"I got you something," Leo interrupted her half-prepared speech and tucked his hand into this jacket opening. He pulled out a heart shaped box and placed it on the table. Its cardboard edges were warped, and the ink had melted the words into a mix of colors from moisture exposure. "I was planning on giving it to you while on the plane, but… you know."

America opened the box lid and peeled back the thin pink cellophane wrapping inside. Foil wrapped chocolate morsels shined under the fluorescent lights and they looked to be dry. She picked a square one and unwrapped it. "I talked to Carol." She placed the rich brown chocolate on her tongue, and it instantly began to melt from the heat the coffee had provided.

"How are things at home?" Leo asked and checked his phone

again. After the last bad news he had gotten through text messaging, she was in no hurry to know what he was looking at.

She put up one finger until she finished chewing the caramel center. "She got in a fight with Pa. Finally."

"Oh, this should be good," he said. "What do you mean by *finally?*"

"You know their past? I guess he pressed her to tell him why she's hated him for so long. The thing is, she's too embarrassed to tell him the truth."

"What's the truth?"

"That she loves him." She picked another chocolate and unwrapped the gold foil. "And she's been in love with him since high school. I've never heard her talk like that. She thought she was protecting herself from getting hurt or hurting others but all she did was close herself off and hurt people, specifically Pa." America played the conversation in her head, picturing what it must have been like all those years for Carol to keep a secret as big as hers, and here she was thinking her little lie about marrying Leo a week early in Vegas was bad. "She saved Pa's life."

"Is that so? By being a thorn in his side." Leo chuckled.

"Her dad was a drunk and had threatened to kill Edwin. That night, the night of the dance, Carol's dad was on a bender and she thought he might actually do it. So, I guess she felt like she had to do what she did that night and forget about him."

Leo's mug shook in his hand. "I had no idea."

"No-one did. She played it off for all these years so well," America said. "I suppose she blames me for cracking her hard exterior. All I know is she loves him, like a lot."

"And Pa?"

"You tell me? You're his best friend."

"I know he loves her too. I think she's the main reason he moved back to the Cove after he got out of the military, and why he stayed long after the water dried up when almost everyone else moved away."

America reached across the table for Leo's hands. His fingers were cold to the touch, and she held them tightly in her palms. "She told me to make things right with you, and that I'll never forgive myself for treating you badly. Leo, I am so sorry for saying that all of this is your fault. It's not. None of it."

Leo dropped her hands and came around to her side of the booth. Their legs touched under the table and his arms circled her shoulders. "Of course, I forgive you, how could I not?"

America hugged him back and felt the weight of her remorse lift from her heart. "You know I love you?"

"I love you so much America Greene—"

"Thorpe," she interrupted with a smirk.

"Thorpe," he repeated and kissed her on the forehead. "I'm so sorry this week hasn't gone how you planned."

"It's hasn't, but to be honest, there's no way I could have planned to accidentally marry the man of my dreams, in Vegas of all places, and then road trip across the country to get home in time for a wedding that people still think is really happening."

America closed her eyes and thought of the past few days. She wasn't usually someone who liked grand romantic gestures, but dinner at the Eiffel Tower was a magical experience that made her feel like the most loved woman in the world. The first night sharing a bed with Leo, her husband, made her feel anxious and all the more loved when he respected her space. The memories of so many wonderful moments forced her to admit that the trip had actually been really nice overall.

"I think the thing weighing on you is the guilt about lying to the people you love." Leo poured another cup of coffee and sipped some. "I haven't had to worry about it, since you've made all the phone calls and I've only texted with Grant about how the retreat is going this week. All business, nothing personal. But you... You've skirted around the truth, and I think it's time to come clean."

"Leo. I can't. My parents will be devastated," she said.

"Are you certain?" Leo asked and checked his phone again.

America couldn't stand not knowing what was holding his attention so acutely. "What do you keep looking at that stupid thing for?"

"I called in a favor to help us out of this. I hope you won't be upset."

"Leo? Why would I be upset?" As the words came out of her mouth, she saw the reasons coming through the front door of the diner. "You called my mom?"

"Texted. But I guess, yes."

America shot a look of disbelief his way as she stood from the table. "Mom, Dad, how are you here?" She hugged them both at the same time and leaned back to look at them. The two people that could help the most were somehow in Buffalo, to be with her.

"We were in the neighborhood," Paul, her father, said with a side grin.

"We landed in Pittsburgh this morning and were driving east when we got Leo's SOS. We headed straight here," Mom said and linked arms with America. "I hear you've had a rough day."

"You don't know the half of it," America said and sat beside Leo.

"I know more than you think," her mom said as the waitress approached.

"Can I get you folks something?" she asked with a pen and notepad in her hands.

"Mom, you should try this lemon curd donut. It's very good."

"I'll have that. And a cup of tea please." Ever since Vivian got back from Italy the previous year, she had preferred tea to coffee, something about the way it reminded her of the leaves on the vineyard vines.

"Anything for you, mister?" The waitress turned to Paul.

"You got anything stronger than coffee?" Paul said with a chuckle. "Club sandwich, and a coke?"

"Coming right up," she said.

"So, you two got hitched in Vegas?" Paul said.

"I guess we're getting right to it," Vivian said and nudged Paul with her elbow into his ribs.

America looked at Leo. "You told them? You went behind my back and against my wishes?"

"Are you actually upset that I did, or do you feel relieved that you don't have to pretend anymore?" Leo asked and held her gaze until she capitulated.

America focused on her mother's face. "I didn't know how to tell you. Plus, you were on a cruise when all this happened. I thought we could just carry on and no one would be any the wiser," she said and held her mom's hand across the table. "I'm sorry I lied about it. It's just that sometimes there's no easy answer."

"The truth is always the easiest way out, dear."

"Your mother's right," Paul said as the waitress placed a soda and water onto the table. "And we're not mad at you in the slightest. So, you got married already, who cares? We are just happy for you both."

"But what about the wedding, all that money?" America whined. "Everyone is looking forward to the big day, and how do I cancel everything this late?"

"We figured, we could still have the ceremony and reception as planned. Maybe we could tell everyone the truth about what happened in Vegas. No harm, no foul. We just don't want to let anyone down," Leo said, and America nodded in agreement.

"What is it that you two want? Really." Vivian asked.

"Earlier I said that I wanted to go back in time and redo the last week of my life, but now..." America looked at Leo and smiled. "I just want to go home, with my husband." Leo mouthed *I love you* and she kissed him lightly on the lips. This man, who swept her off her feet and made her see herself through a new lens, not the version she thought people wanted to see but the real America. She wanted nothing more than to get him alone, with a bottle of wine, and a good romcom on the TV. What she craved now, more than ever, was a normal day.

"The wedding is two days away. If you want to move forward with your plan, your father and I will help keep your secret, though I don't know how long before someone finds out. You know how small towns are. But if that's what you want to do…"

"And there's the magazine to consider," America said remembering that all the couples who got married alongside them were to be listed in the next issue.

"Well, if we can't have it, why don't we just give the wedding to Carol and Pa. Solve everyone's problems," Leo laughed but America didn't find it funny.

"That's not a bad idea," Vivian said. She looked up to the ceiling as though she might find the answer written there.

"Wait. I was totally joking," Leo said and mumbled through a backtrack of what he had just suggested.

Considering her mom and Leo, America ran scenarios in her mind about how it could work. She could call Carol and they could hatch a plan together to surprise Pa. All the same people would be there whether it was America and Leo, or Carol and Pa getting married. After all, they were already the best man and maid of honor for the ceremony. It could work.

"I know that look," Paul said as his towering sandwich arrived. He clapped his fingers together and grinned at the plate of food. "Sandwich time."

"And who's gonna tell Carol and Pa?" Leo said, probably regretting having spurred the women's imaginations on.

CHAPTER 21

Having dropped their broken-into, over-priced rental car off in Buffalo, the foursome carpooled to a cute bed and breakfast a few hours closer to home. On recommendation from a friend of Paul's, America's father secured two rooms in a place near Rome for the night where America got right to work.

Running down the staircase, America squealed the good news. "You guys. She's in!" She turned through the arched cased opening and realized her party wasn't alone in the sitting room. "Sorry," she said in a more restrained tone to the elderly couple reading beside the fireplace. She tiptoed the remaining steps to where her parents and Leo sat at a game table beside the window. "Carol said all we need to do is show up, act like everything is normal. She's got it from there."

"How did she take the news?" Mom asked.

"I think somehow, she already knew. It seemed like she wasn't surprised at all and kind of giggled when I told her what happened in Las Vegas," America said and mimicked the little laugh. "I've never heard her so giddy. Anyway, When I realized that everyone is going to know the truth once my article is published, the deception wouldn't have worked, and now everyone will get the big wedding event they want."

"You could still have just told everyone and still had the reception to celebrate with everyone," Paul said while shuffling a deck of cards.

"I see that now. I think I just wanted everything to be so perfect and really impress everyone in town that I lost sight of what the wedding day is all about. But don't worry. This is going to be so much better."

"I can tell you're feeling better about this," Leo said as she sat sideways on his lap, even though there was a vacant chair at the table. "What are you going to do for a dress? I feel so bad that you won't be able to wear it. I bet you would have looked magnificent in it."

She nuzzled his neck and kissed his cheek. "We'll never know."

Vivian put her hand up like she was a student in a classroom. "Why don't I call that great little shop in Elizabethtown where I got my dress and see what they have on short notice. You're a sample size anyway, maybe they have something that'll work."

Before America could protest, her mother shot from her seat and took her phone from her pocket. Her eyes lit up at having something to do to contribute after being out of touch for the last week.

What a week it had been! The morning had been a wild coaster ride. Finding freedom in telling the truth, so much had changed inside America. Though the road to Saturday was paved a little smoother now, she suspected the next few days would be just as eventful as the previous ones. Surrounded by her favorite people, gratitude warmed her heart. "I still can't believe you guys met up with us. I don't know how you did it."

America's dad sipped an amber liquid, some variety of scotch, and placed the glass on a cork coaster. "It just so happened that

Leo texted us and we were able to swing on over. We weren't really in the neighborhood so to speak, but a couple hours detour was worth it if we could help."

"I'm really glad you're here, Dad," America said and shook his hand. She leaned her head on Leo's shoulder. "And thank you for calling them in. I guess even when you're grown, sometimes you just need your parents."

Vivian came back from the front hall where she had made the phone call, and a broad smile puffed her cheeks. Her enthusiasm was impossible to miss. "Good news. The shop said they have a couple gowns in your size, and they will hold them for us for you to try on tomorrow. We can swing by on our way to the Cove and get it. Isn't that fantastic?"

"Mom, what if they're all hideous?"

"So what? You wear the least horrid thing and slap a smile on your face. Understood?" she said like any mother would.

America nodded. Her mother was a great many things, not least of all a take-charge-type-A woman. If there was a problem needing solving, Vivian was right there in the thick of things. America wouldn't have put it past her mother to have concocted this whole mess, just to have something productive to do.

"What's so funny, babe?" Leo spoke softly into her ear.

"I'll tell you later."

"Like when I finally get you alone tonight?"

America's cheeks warmed as she nodded, barely able to hide her grin.

Paul began to deal the cards out and Leo waved him off. "I think I'm ready to knock off."

"What about you, America?" Paul asked with a hopeful pump of his brows to have another player.

"I'm ready to crash too. Maybe a bath first," America said and pretended to nod off.

Paul restacked the cards. "Vi?" She shook her head, and he

realized his hopes for a good round of spades were gone. "Anything else you need us to arrange for Saturday?" Paul added. "You don't have to do everything by yourself."

"There is one little thing," America said. "We didn't mention this earlier, but we don't have a cake anymore."

Leo chimed in. "The storm knocked out the power at the bakery. Just think melted cakes, defrosted refrigerators, and a colorful flood in the building. A disaster zone."

"Can Alfonso whip something up?" Paul asked.

"I don't feel right about adding anything to his already full plate. As it is, he's still got Foundry guests to feed until they check out tomorrow, then he has to switch gears and prepare all the food for the reception."

"Speaking of Alfonso, I wonder what Carol and Pa picked out at the tasting the other day? I didn't really ask," America said. "I guess this whole *letting go of control* thing isn't too bad after all."

"No worries about the cake. I've got it covered."

"Thanks Mom."

"I'm only glad that everything is working out now." Mom wrapped her arms around America and patted Leo on the shoulders. "I almost forgot. We sent a little something up to your room."

What could it be? America wondered. "Thanks?" she said with suspicion in her pitched tone.

"We're gonna turn in soon. See you at breakfast tomorrow."

Lifting America off his lap, Leo took her by the hand and escorted her up the curved staircase. He took out the old skeleton key with a silk tassel hanging from the top and unlocked the door to room number seven. Inside, a small cart was positioned next to the fireplace. A fluffy white fur blanket was draped over a pink settee with a wooden frame that screamed cozy luxury. The surprise was waiting on the cart; a bottle of sweet sparkling wine and a platter of cheeses, and chocolates.

"This is exactly what I needed after today," America said, and pulled Leo inside the door. With her arms wrapped around his neck, and her lips planted on his, she kicked the door shut with her heel.

CHAPTER 22

America exhaled a deep breath as they rolled back into town. Decisively home, after the longest drive ever, there was still much for her to do, and someone she needed to see. Her parents had dropped them off at the station where Leo's truck had been parked and took their own car into Christmas Cove slightly ahead of them.

Climbing down from Leo's truck, she handed the newly picked out dress, securely hidden inside a black nylon dress bag, to her mom. Unlike the beautiful, though not practical, satin wedding dress bag, this one would keep her new gown clean. Luck had kissed her at the dress shop in Elizabethtown when she tried on the most unexpected of choices and it fit her perfectly. Her selection was sure to make waves at the wedding tomorrow, she amused herself imagining the looks on the guests' faces.

Thankfully, since her parents showed up in Buffalo, all the things that had been going wrong were now being righted. Though her parents were helping with the logistical issues, one person deserved all the credit for setting America straight. Her husband, who had known what she needed before she even realized it herself, demonstrated his love in all the ways that would ever matter.

"Can you believe we're really doing this?" America said to Leo who was unloading the rest of their luggage from the bed of his old, red truck. "Do you mind finishing up here? I need to run across the street to Carol's and work out some details for tomorrow."

Leo gave her a quick kiss and nodded. "I have a call to make too, though I should probably go in person."

"Pa?"

"I'm guessing he needs a friend about now," Leo said. "I'll see you later."

Knowing that Leo was so centered gave America the mental breathing room that she needed to pull off the biggest surprise of her life. She hurried to Carol's house across Main Street, but down a little from where America's pink, mid-reno, Victorian house was. Upon arriving at Carol's front door, she noticed that all the snow had been removed from the stoop and the door itself appeared cleaner than usual, which meant Carol had been stress cleaning recently.

America knocked, and Carol opened the door as though she had been waiting for her arrival.

Carols arms flew around America's shoulders, and she hugged her while standing in the door opening. "Come in. I've been expecting you for hours." Carol shuffled them inside and took America's coat.

She wore a pencil skirt and a red turtleneck sweater because all of her other clothes were dirty with many items having been worn multiple times. America discreetly smelled herself just to make sure she wasn't going to offend the older woman's sensibilities.

"Tea? I made cookies too," Carol walked through the sparkling formal sitting room into the kitchen. "I didn't sleep again last night because I'm too excited."

"Oh?" America said, urging Carol to continue. She walked around the tufted sofa to the built-in shelves on the far side where books, new and old, were intermixed with dozens of framed photos. There was not a speck of dust on any of the items, which confirmed her suspicions that Carol had been cleaning.

"I'm just so nervous about tomorrow. All those people are going to stare, and what if Edwin is too shocked to say yes?" Carol said and banged around in the kitchen. Teacups clanged against plates and silverware tinkled onto the tabletop. "This darn stove!"

"Do you need help, Carol?"

Carol growled at something. "Nope. I'll be right there."

America giggled and thought about how far her friend had come in the little over a year since their first meeting. The woman who was known as Scrooge McCarol because of her general unpleasant comportment, had morphed into a vivacious and funny woman. She seemed to be years younger now than she had appeared only months earlier. And when Carol walked back into the parlor, balancing a golden tray with all the tea fixings on top, she was positively glowing.

"Here, let me help you." America took the tray and placed it on the glass coffee table by the sofa. "You have nothing to be nervous about. You love Pa, and I have it under good authority that he loves you too. What do you have to lose by proclaiming it in front of the whole town?"

"My prickly reputation?" Carol chuckled, though her nerves were clear on her tense face.

"Sit. I'll pour."

Carol's bum hit the edge of the cushion and then she popped right up again, startling America. "What is it?" America asked and dabbed the spilled water with a cloth napkin.

"You want to see the dress?"

"Sure. Right now?"

"Why not? Got nothing else to do." Carol ran up the steps, taking them by twos, and hurried back down with a dress bag dragging behind her.

America had never seen Carol so spun up and didn't even think it was possible for her to be so animated. Hiding a giggle behind the sound of swirling the spoon in the teacup, she watched Carol unzip the garment bag. Even though America had seen the dress when Carol initially tried it on months ago, she couldn't quite recall what the details looked like.

Carol flung the dress out and held it up like a big catch. Her worry lines disappeared with the raising of her brows. "Can anxiety kill me? Because my heart is racing right now at what Edwin will think."

"Didn't he already see you in the dress this week?"

"What's your point? He's never seen me walking down an aisle before. And since he's the best man, he'll be at the front, standing with Leo." Carol fluffed the bottom frilly layer and held it up to her torso. Spinning around like a young girl, she smiled and breathed deeply.

"You really are happy, aren't you?" America said and stood in front of Carol. She took the dress and draped it over a blue wingback chair and took Carol's hands. "You will be fine."

"I can't believe I let you talk me into doing this."

"You love him?"

Carol nodded and her eyes glassed over.

"And you're done holding onto the pain of your past?"

She nodded again.

"You know that your father's mistakes were never yours to hold onto in the first place, right? You deserve to be truly happy, and on your own terms." America hugged Carol for a moment. "Now that we have that understood, what is the plan for tomorrow?"

"That's easy. Everything will proceed as though you and Leo are still having the wedding, but when you get to the end of the aisle, I'll take it from there. Do you trust me?" Carol said with a devious grin that should have scared America, but only piqued her curiosity more.

"I'm ready. Leo is ready. Mom and Dad know what's going on. And Pa?"

"He's used to thinking on his toes. I think he'll figure out what's really going on quick enough. But..." Carol paused, and her face deflated. "What if he says no?"

"I don't think that'll happen. But if it does, you slap a smile on your face, understood?" America repeated her mom's earlier advice about a possible hideous dress, and hoped it was enough to work in this situation too.

"And then say something snarky and self-deprecating?" Carol smiled again, though America knew she was deflecting her real feelings.

"If that's what feels right in the moment." She rubbed her hands up and down the back of Carol's arms to reassure her. "Now, I need to get out of here to do some laundry and take a shower." America headed to the door. "I'm right across the street if you need me, okay?"

"I can't believe we're going to do this, but I feel better now that you're actually back. Thank you for rushing over here." Carol said as America opened the front door. "Oh, and I almost forgot. Congratulations."

"Thanks, Carol," America said and kissed both of Carol's cheeks. "See you tomorrow."

CHAPTER 23

With two cups of cider in hand, Leo walked down the hall that led from the kitchen at the rear of America's house to the formal parlor, which was one of the only completed rooms in her fixer-upper Victorian. He hated how long the renovation had taken so far, but they had both put far more energy into getting The Foundry up and going than they had into finishing her home. He passed the framed photos of their adventures hanging on the exposed lath board and was reminded that this was now *his* home too.

Even though America acquired the property before their engagement, he had somehow always known that he would live here someday. Now that they were married, he could finally move out of his trailer and into an actual house, although wishing for a draft-free structure was apparently too much to ask for at this point in his life. With The Foundry resort running smoothly and bringing in a profit, he could finally invest in making the house their home.

"What are you smiling about?" America asked as he came into the light of the fireplace. His contentment must have been showing.

Leo handed her a mug and sat beside her on the one new piece of furniture they had purchased together, a leather chesterfield sofa. She had liked it for its rich historic look, while he had liked the tobacco color that reminded him of his dad smoking his favorite cigars. Whatever their reasons, he was satisfied to let the warm leather hug him in.

"I was just thinking about how perfect this house is for us. Or it will be when we finish it," Leo said and clinked his mug against hers. "I can just picture us sitting here, little kids running circles around a beautiful Christmas tree, hosting grand parties, and loving you more every day." He liked the way his words excited America and blushed her cheeks.

"Is that right?" she said. "And what else have you been imagining since I saw you five minutes ago?"

"I saw us sitting by the fire and laughing ourselves to sleep, me carrying you up the stairs to our bedroom, and—"

She stopped him with a kiss, which did less than she probably hoped to quell his musings. "I get the idea."

"Are you ready for tomorrow? It's going to be crazy."

"It's nuts," America said. "I can't believe we're going to do this. Carol is a ball of nerves, and I must admit, I am too. what if Pa says no to her?"

"He won't," Leo said and bit back his own grin.

"Leopold, what did you do?" she said with her hand propped on her hip the way he liked.

His hands went up as though to say he didn't do anything, but the truth was itching to escape. "I warned Pa, and he... He gave me something." Leo walked to the foyer where his coat hung on a nail on the wall and returned with a dainty box covered in faded golden velvet. "He's been carting this thing around since Desert Storm."

Leo handed her the box. She hesitated, bewilderment glazing her eyes. The box creaked and opened uneasily in her fingers. "It's a ring?" America presented the contents to him as though he hadn't yet seen the silver engagement ring with a yellow stone propped up at the center.

"He planned to propose when he made it home from the war, but when he got back, he was met with a cold and sour version of the woman he loved."

"And he held onto it this whole time?"

"Now you know why I had to warn him about tomorrow. Pa knows Carol is planning something romantic for him after our vows, and he wants to be ready to beat her to the punch."

America laughed. "That sounds just like them." America sipped her drink and stood in front of the fire. "I'm relieved that she won't be humiliated in front of everyone, and I feel a little less guilty about keeping all of this a secret."

"I think it will all turn out fine. We just need a good night's rest, America Thorpe," Leo said and watched her place her mug on the white-painted wood mantel.

She looked into the gold framed mirror hanging on the wall above the fire, and the reflection of her eyes smoldered at him, tempting him. She unpinned her hair from the top of her head, and her long dark waves cascaded down her back. She wore a blush pink satin pajama set and fluffy white slippers, and she took his breath away.

Leo stood and went to her, letting his fingers glide over the soft fabric around her back. She turned her head towards him, but her back stayed pressed against his stomach. Standing behind her, he wet his lips with anticipation. She turned her head and brushed her warm pillowy mouth across his. Reaching his other arm around her front, he encircled her waist, pulling her hips against his. Her breath caught at the tug. He moved her hair away from her neck so he could feel her jawline against his mouth, and he peppered kisses down her nape and along the line of her shoulder.

"Leo," she whispered his name with her eyes closed.

Her little moan sent a thrill down his spine. This incredible woman was *his* to have and hold, and he planned on having her right now. He took her hand and led her out of the room towards the stairs, but a pounding on the door stopped them both on the bottom step. "You've got to be kidding me," Leo said. "Why don't you head up, and I'll get rid of whoever it is."

America pouted as she let go of his hand and climbed the steps behind him. He opened the door, and in flew a curly red-haired ball of energy, screaming excitement. "Hello, Poppy," he said as she barely gave him a hurried side hug while pushing her way inside.

"Where is that beautiful bride?" Poppy, America's former assistant at the magazine and all-around best friend, said. She was one of those people that he liked but couldn't keep up with, and right now, she was poking her head into the first room. "America? Helloooo," she sang out.

America peeked around the banister at the top of the steps, "Poppy, is that you?"

Leo nodded from where he stood like roadkill in the foyer and pointed his open hand toward the kitchen to where Poppy had gone next. "That way."

"Sorry," America mouthed as she ran down the stairs and flung herself around the newel post.

Poppy skipped back down the hallway toward the foyer, and Leo could do nothing but watch the two women collide into each other's embrace. Supposing it was time for a cold shower and glass of whisky, he poked his head out the front door just to make certain there were no more surprise guests coming to ruin his otherwise peaceful evening.

It was the jingling bells and horse hooves clopping on the cobblestone road that caused Leo to walk down the front steps and brick path. Looking down the road, he shook his head at the sight coming his way. Pa stood center stage in the carriage, holding Bingo's reins. Pa's horse was somewhat of a town celebrity and had become a bonafide mascot in recent years.

Leo wasn't even embarrassed to consider the large animal a friend.

Leo wrapped his cardigan around his torso and approached the curb as Pa pulled up. "What's going on?"

Pa jumped down to the street. His absence exposed a horde of men who raised their steins and shouted Leo's name. Cam, one of Leo's closest friends, reached out and shook Leo's hand.

"What the heck are you guys doing here?" Leo said and shook his brother, John's, hand. "I'm a little surprised to see you here tonight."

"I wouldn't want to miss this, little brother. After the year we've had, I hope I've shown you that I mean no ill towards you," John said and pulled Leo in for a double shoulder tap bro hug. "Plus, who doesn't like a bachelor party?"

Leo's eyes pushed back into his brain as he grasped what was happening. His worst nightmare. "I don't have a choice, do I? I just drove across the country with a somewhat grouchy bridezilla, got a flat tire in St. Louis, got snowed in in Buffalo, saw an empty Niagara Falls, got my credit card declined. My car was broken into, and I finally got home a few hours ago. I mean, we canceled the rehearsal tonight because we're exhausted."

"That's yesterday's problems, Leopold. Time to suit up!" Cam said.

"Yeah, we don't care how tired you are," Grant, the operations manager at The Foundry, said.

Alfonso poked his head around with a silly grin. "Alfonso not know what tonight is." He held his stein and cheered towards the starry sky. "*Buona salute.*"

A hand patted Leo on his shoulder from behind and he spun around on the heel of his slippers. "Paul? You knew about this?"

Paul, who clearly knew that the two were already married, leaned in, and whispered. "I got you covered." He stood back and held up two pairs of hockey skates and a duffle bag. "Now, what are we doing standing around here?"

Grant and Alfonso, who remained in the carriage lifted their hockey sticks over their heads like trophies and shouted. "Let's go!"

Luckily, the revelry didn't startle Bingo, who Pa expertly led out of town. Leo had only one clue as to the evening's festivities, hockey somewhere. In the meantime, there was plenty to drink from a mini keg of what he could only assume was one of Pa's potions.

"You excited for the big day?" Cam asked. "I remember when Jenny and I got hitched. It was the most stressful day of my life, up until little Charlotte was born. Having a baby is a whole other world of stress."

Leo nodded but had no time to properly answer before Grant chimed in. "My wedding wasn't stressful, just really relaxing."

"Maybe that was because of how hung over you were, or maybe because your bride was stressed enough for the two of you," John joked, though he himself had never been married, and would therefore have no basis for his presumptions. Leo motioned with a swipe at his neck for John to not continue down his current thought path. John likely was not aware that Grant's first wife had passed away not long after they were married.

"Maybe the next time will be different, and you can have all the stress you deserve," Leo said. "Is there going to be a next time?"

Grant hesitated too long before answering, and the company went wild.

"When are you gonna ask her?" Cam said.

"Ask who what?" Alfonso chimed in.

"Thandie," Leo said and grabbed Alfonso's shoulders. "He's in love with Thandie."

As the news clicked, Alfonso's eyes widened. "Grant and Thandie, from work? Alfonso not see this coming."

"Because you're always in the *cucina*," Paul said and slapped him over the back. "What about you, Pa?" Cam asked. "Got your eye on anyone special?"

"You know I'm too old for all this love stuff," Pa said and kept his eyes trained forward on the dark gravel road. The carriage was outfitted with one single headlight that only lit twenty feet or so in front of Bingo. "And I don't think I'm the dating type."

"But the marrying type maybe?" Leo said, already knowing the answer.

Pa shrugged. "I'll never tell," he said like a peevish child, and urged Bingo forward.

Leo chuckled in his throat. Even though he was more tired than he knew was possible, he was glad to have these men in his life. As to what they were up to, he was putting the pieces together. The carriage crested the road, he knew all too well, that led to The Foundry. With all the resort guests having checked out earlier in the day, the place was way too quiet, but the large crystal chandelier hanging inside the renovated barn, shined through the two-story windows and lit the parking area.

The Harbour House was still one of his favorite places to be. America had taken on much of the design, and he hoped their home would be just as nice and peaceful when that renovation was eventually finished.

Pa pulled the carriage to a stop in front of the building. He hopped down and tied off Bingo's lines.

"Well, men, shall the party commence?" Cam said and jumped down to the ground without spilling a drop of beer from his stein.

The word *commence* frightened Leo more than it should have, and he chalked it up to how tired he was. "Let's do... whatever this is."

CHAPTER 24

"I thought you weren't coming in until tomorrow," America said. Rubbing sleepiness from her eyes, she pulled out a wood spindle chair, that definitely needed replacing, from the kitchen table.

Poppy waved it off, indicating she wasn't going to sit. "I know that's what I told you, but I had to come now. I brought something you might need."

"Curious," America said as the front door squeaked open. "I don't know what Leo is up to. It's freezing out there."

Though America was unable to see down the hallway from her spot at the table, Poppy leaned her head around the kitchen doorway. "That's not Leo."

"Who is it then?" America stood and mimicked Poppy's stance.

The front door opened, and America's mom was coming through, backside first. "Can I get some help with this door?" she called to them.

America and Poppy ran up to the front of the house. America held the door open while Poppy helped carry whatever was in her mom's hands.

"Careful," Vivian said and turned around holding a beautiful white cake.

"Mom, did you make this?"

She laughed. "Are you kidding? You've had my cakes before, and I don't think you want me to serve one to a hundred guests. You have Poppy to thank for bringing this."

America looked at the square box base and saw the logo from her favorite bakery from back in the city. "How did you know?"

Poppy and Vivian walked the two-tier cake back to the kitchen while America looked out into the front lawn for any sign of Leo. She followed them down the hall and inspected the round layers. Tiny pink and red flowers glittered like morning dew around the base of each layer and small green pearls dotted the surface like little leaves. It was nearly as pretty as the one she and Leo had originally picked out and a miracle that Poppy had gotten one on such short notice.

"Your mom called me yesterday and told me what happened at the local bakery, so I headed over to The Frankery in your old neighborhood and begged Frank for a rush order for his favorite customer," Poppy said and embraced America. "He always did like you."

"I'll have to thank him in person next time I'm in town.," America said and hugged her mom too. "Thank you for doing this."

"You can't have a wedding without cake," Vivian said and winked. "Oh, I forgot to tell you, Leo is out with your father."

"I wondered where he had run off to. Poppy showed up and it was like he disappeared. What are they doing?"

"At this exact moment, I don't know," Vivian said with a wink.

America was immediately suspicious of the cagey way her mother answered. "What are you not telling me?" She turned to her friend, "Poppy, what do you know? This better not be some other grand romantic scheme. I'm too tired for that."

Poppy and Vivian shrugged in unison.

"Okay, I'm on to you two. What are you conspiring about? I know you could have just brought the cake up from town tomorrow morning. So, what is all this?"

"Nothing," Poppy said. "I just decided to come early. You know, because of the weather I didn't want to push my luck tomorrow and run into a situation."

Still suspicious, but glad her friend was there, America just wanted to sit by the fire and catch up. "Well, let's go get your luggage and get you settled. You can stay in the guest room as long as you're alright dodging boxes of tile and flooring samples."

"No need," Poppy said. "I'm already over at your mom's for the night. I didn't want to impose or stress you out the night before your wedding. There's one more thing I have to tell you. Wait here." Poppy ran to the front door where a group of high-pitched voices filled the foyer.

America looked at Mom, "Is this really happening? I'm so tired," she whined.

"It's happening. Sorry. I had to go along with it to help keep the ruse going."

America rolled her eyes, though she shouldn't have been so irritated at how thoughtful her friends were. She left the kitchen and joined the group of women gathered in the foyer.

"Surprise!" Jenny, Cam's wife, said and came in holding two bottles of prosecco. "The party has officially arrived!"

Jenny had become one of America's closest friends in town, not because she was one of the few people in town that was of her same generation, but she was absolutely the sweetest and most thoughtful neighbor. Cam, her husband also happened to be one of Leo's best friends. And if that wasn't enough of a reason, she had been sorority sisters with Thandie back in college. Jenny had suggested that Thandie might be the right person for the job as the activities director down at The Foundry, and after a year on the job, it was clear that she had not been wrong.

Coming in behind Jenny, Thandie's bright smile shined from under the shadow of her signature baseball cap. "Hey, beautiful. We decided we can't let you get married without a little get together with your best girlfriends." Thandie was one of those women who was naturally good at all sorts of things and had an enviable confidence. She was someone that America had leaned on more than once over the previous few months of stressful wedding planning.

"I'm glad to see you," America said and embraced Thandie. "You'll never believe me when I tell you the kind of week I had."

"Well, I want to hear all about it, but not right now," Thandie said. "Whatever it is, can wait."

Vivian wrapped her arms over Thandie and Jenny's shoulders, saving America from saying too much in the process. "Is everything ready?"

Thandie checked her watch. "We're gonna be late if we don't get going."

America looked down at her wrist where her timepiece usually fit, but she had taken it off when dressing for bed earlier. Now she wished she were heading to bed instead of entertaining her friends. "Where are we going?" America asked in a sulking tone. "Don't get me wrong, I'm very happy you're all here, but I. Am. Exhausted."

Just as America was going to give another excuse, Carol came bounding up the front steps with a travel mug of something steamy in her hand. She thrust the drink into America's hand and the scent of warm, spiced coffee filled her nose. "Nutmeg pecan," Carol said. "Drink it."

It seemed as though America had no choice in whatever their plan was for the evening. "What time is it anyway?" she asked Thandie.

"Seven fifteen."

"Seriously? It feels closer to eleven," she said. "Can you have jetlag from a car ride?"

"Not a thing," Poppy giggled.

Badly wishing she was in bed with her husband, but realizing she was outnumbered, America looked down at her pink pajamas. "You all are dressed like you're going on an arctic expedition. Should I get changed?"

"Something warm," Jenny said and opened one of the prosecco bottles. She took a swig directly from the opening and handed it to Carol, who did the same.

With a chuckle in her throat, America began up the stairs. "I'll be right back down."

"We'll be waiting outside," Thandie said. "And hurry."

America dug through her drawers and pulled out a pair of pink fleece leggings, a cream-colored waffle knit turtleneck, and a close-fitting red hoodie. She threw on the items and grabbed her coat on the way out the front door. Outside, the air was crisp and cool, and her breath condensed, making little cloud shapes in front of her face.

"Come on, get in," Jenny said from the front seat of her minivan.

America's mom pointed at Jenny to get out of the driver's seat and switched places with the tipsy woman with little complaint. In the backseat, the sparkling wine was passed around and they all took turns drinking straight from the bottle like uncivilized deviants. America took a big gulp and felt the cold sharp bubbles sink down her throat. It was gonna be a wild night by all indications, and she smiled as she looked around the cabin at her favorite people. Who cares if she already got married, they would find out soon enough and she would have no regrets about missing out on traditional wedding events like a bachelorette party.

"Did you have any idea we were surprising you tonight?" Poppy asked.

"None. I thought Leo and I were just going to have a nice quiet pre-wedding evening. Where is he anyway?" Everyone shrugged suspiciously. "Mom, do you know?"

"I told you, he's with your father."

"Why do I feel like there's more going on here?" America said and watched out the window to determine where they were heading. The gravel road gave it away. "What's happening at The Foundry?"

Jenny and Thandie, seated in the far back row, laughed about something which only caused America to be more curious. "Tell me, will ya?"

"Patience. You'll find out in about ninety seconds," Thandie said, and America wondered which one of them was more neurotic about tracking the time.

Ninety seconds wasn't too much to wait. She used the time to calm her nerves with a few more swigs and peered out into the night. The van came over the newly installed covered bridge, lit by the little lights strung along the eaves, and into The Foundry parking lot. All the lights were on inside the building and illuminated the whole driveway. Outside the entry door, she spotted her favorite horse.

"Bingo's here? Whatever for?" America clapped and was anxious to greet her furry friend. "Are we going on some sort of sleighride?" America opened the sliding door and hopped out first.

"Get back in here," Vivian said and pulled the van alongside America as she walked towards the front doors. Poppy reached out and tugged her back inside the vehicle like she was being kidnapped. Vivian pressed the gas and continued past the main building and down the narrow road leading to the lake without even closing the van door.

The headlights bounced off of the bright white snow and ice in front of them. America was surprised the lake still held some water since last spring's rains, especially after it had been dry for so long beforehand. An expert came in during the fall to assess the reasons and long-term viability of the Cove retaining its water. Years of healthy wildflower and tall grass growth had created a dense root structure below the sediments. And like a tightly woven canvas, the water stayed.

Their frozen little lake was beautiful. The sight of men dancing around the bonfire on the lakeshore was unexpected.

CHAPTER 25

With the headlights shining across cleared ice, the girls piled out of the van and joined the men by the bonfire. America spotted her dad chatting with Pa, who were about the same age. Coming between them, Leo draped his arms around both older men and caused a riotous laugh. John, Leo's brother chatted up Cam, who stopped the conversation when his wife, Jenny stumbled down the shore.

"Whoa, Jenny," Cam said and took her under his arm. Cam kissed her on the lips but pulled back from her just as fast as he had dived in. "Whoa, babe! How much did you drink?"

Jenny held up the nearly empty bottle and giggled.

"All that?" Cam asked, his concerned squinted eyes glinted in the firelight.

America stepped up to save her. "She barely had any. We've all been sharing it."

"Listen to me, Cameron Townsend." Jenny poked a finger into Cam's chest, depressing the puffy coat. "I'm not used to it. I only weaned Charlotte a couple weeks ago. And it's a party. What's a girl supposed to do?"

"She's got a fair point, Cam," America said and took Jenny's hand. "I'll handle this."

Leo met them and handed Jenny a bottle of water. "Can you believe this?" he whispered to America as he leaned in to peck her cheek.

She shook her head back and forth. "This is wild," she said as she watched all of her favorite people gathered together in one place. Even though she just wanted to be in bed, the evening was likely to be an unforgettable one.

Thandie, always the director, stood on a wooden bench made out of cut tree stumps and wooden planks, and clapped her hands to get their attention. "We're all here tonight to celebrate these two gorgeous humans on the eve of their wedding. I think I can speak for all of us here when I say that we want nothing more than for you two to have a wonderful life together. We love you."

As the group clapped and cheered, Leo pulled America into his chest. With an arm behind her back, he dipped her low and pressed his lips to hers. She loved the overly dramatic show of their affection and wondered just how much *he* had had to drink since being kidnapped. She, however, did not mind the feel of his pillowy mouth pressing into hers, tipsy or not.

"Alright. Alright, you two. Enough of the lovey-dovey stuff," Thandie said.

Leo finished kissing her properly and came up for air, righting America and balancing her with a hand on the small of her back. "If it wasn't for a bonfire like this one, I don't know if any of us would be here celebrating tonight," Leo said and moved his thumb along her spine.

The memory of the Bonfire of the Fears flooded America's mind. Her heart warmed as she realized just how correct Leo was. They had written their fears on scraps of paper and thrown in them into the flames with the hope of being released from whatever held them back. "Good thing we're such bad shots or I don't know if we would have ever told each other the truth."

"That I want to spend the rest of my life with you?" Leo said and rubbed the tip of his nose against hers.

"I guess we have this bonfire to thank too," Thandie said, stealing their attention back to herself. Little glowing embers fell from the sky around her and the fire acted like a spotlight on her tan skin. From behind Thandie, Grant leaned in and nudged his elbow into the side of her leg. She smiled broadly, her lips framing enviable pretty teeth, before hardening her features at him. "Enough of this happy talk. This isn't a time for peace. It's time for battle!" She growled the last word and caused them all to chuckle.

"Is that so?" Grant hopped up onto the bench beside Thandie and bumped her off with his hip. "This bachelor and bachelorette party isn't your traditional event."

"There's no strippers," Thandie teased. "Sorry, boys."

"And there's no relaxing spa treatments. Sorry, ladies." Grant ran his hand down his face and took the smug look with it. "Here's the deal. Boys against girls. Five-minute periods. No goalies. No checking. No penalty shots. In the case of a tie, which there won't be because—"

Thandie pulled on Grant's waistband from behind and took his place on the stump. "Because the girls are gonna win. We'll have a shoot-out. Everyone clear?"

"But the guys have one more person than the girls," America said and counted the teams out loud with her fingers to make sure. "Me, Poppy, Carol, Thandie, Jenny, and Mom. Leo, Grant, Cam, John, Pa, Dad, and Alfonso."

"Alfonso no skate." The animated chef held his hands up beside his face and wiggled his fingers. "Shake my money makers, no?"

Everyone laughed along with the young Italian who had come to work at The Foundry a year ago. Vivian had befriended the man during a trip to northern Italy the previous Christmas. When Leo decided to transform the old lake houses into an upscale retreat, Alfonso was at the top of his mind to join the team. America was glad to see him embracing new experiences, but the hockey game would be better with even teams.

"Maybe Alfonso could be the ref?" she suggested.

"Great idea," Grant said and tossed a glowing, chartreuse hockey puck in Alfonso's direction. "Nice catch. When we're ready to start, just drop that thing on the ice between the centers and then get the heck out of the way as fast as you can."

"Now that that's settled. Let's get to the good stuff," Poppy said. "What do the girls get when we win?" and America admired her confidence in the girls' abilities.

"The stakes. I almost forgot," Thandie said. "The losers will be on Bingo's stable duty for the next month, and the winners, the girls obviously—"

"The winners will win bragging rights and the pool," Grant finished her sentence.

"What's the pool?" Leo said.

Grant grabbed an old rusty coffee can from beside the fire and held it up. "Everyone get whatever cash you have on you right now and shove it in here. Winners take all!"

"I have all the equipment laid out over there," Thandie pointed to a pile of skates and sticks stuck into the piled-up snow. "Let's go to war, people!"

The men and women separated as they grabbed their gear, and there was no fraternizing with the enemy. America was surprised to see Carol lacing up her skates in one fluid motion like a pro. Poppy needed help with hers, and Jenny was kind enough to assist.

"I've never played hockey before," Vivian said to Carol, who sat on either side of America.

"But you've skated before," America said.

Thandie leaned over from further down the bench. "I've

gotten a ton of time on this ice over the last few weeks with the guests. I mean, how cool was it that we got to have a Christmas Eve skate this year?"

"I can't believe all that water level stayed through the summer and fall," Carol said. "It hasn't been like this in a really long time."

"Do you think we'll have the lake full for the summer again?" Jenny said. "The water activities will bring a lot more people to town."

The whole town had felt the stress since the dam blew out and the lake dried up, but these past few months had brought a renewed outlook to the Cove. In the year since the neighboring city, Elizabethtown, had incorporated Christmas Cove, it wasn't much more than a name and a feeling. But with the population doubling since then, they would have the opportunity for a voting member of the council, and perhaps an alderman in coming years. Things were definitely improving all around town, including Leo's strained relationship with his brother.

Across the ice, Leo sat next to John. They were laughing about something—she wished she could hear what was so humorous—but it was nice to see them getting along. America finished wrapping her laces and grabbed a stick from where they had been stabbed into mounded snow around the makeshift rink space. In the same snow heap, someone had nestled a keg and a couple bottles of unopened booze.

Grant half-buried the coffee can and stood like a club bouncer at the entrance to the cleared ice. "Cough it up," Grant said and folded his arms in front of his chest.

America dug in her coat pocket and flashed a crisp twenty-dollar bill in front of Grant's face.

"Is that all? These stakes are no joke," he teased, and she swiped her fingers over the paper revealing two more bills.

"Is this better?" She crammed the money into the can and snapped her fingers in a taunting way. Pushing him aside and gliding across the ice, she knew this hockey game was going to be worth staying up for. Taking a turn around the makeshift rink, she found her comfort stride as the others did the same. Everyone was finding their legs, except Poppy who was struggling to stay up on her feet at the entrance.

America skated over to her, but John got to Poppy first. He reached down to help her, but she dismissed his hand. Instead, she dug in her blade edge and pushed him away. "Accept no mercy. Give no quarter," she yelled a war cry which elicited an echo of female shouts. Hockey game or not, it was no surprise for Poppy to react to John in that way. She had been holding a grudge against the mayor of Elizabethtown for over a year. Poppy was a loyal friend, and there was no way she was going to forgive John for what he did to Leo, until Leo was ready to forgive him first.

Concerned for his safety, America put herself between John and Poppy before her loyalty turned violent. "Save it for the game," she said and helped Poppy, who was showing off just how much of a city girl she really was. "The trick is to keep your weight centered over the blade. Not too far forward or too far back. Then use the edge to press into the ice and you'll go forward."

Poppy turned and shot eyeball fingers at John, threatening him that she was keeping her eyes on him. "I just can't with that man."

"You know Leo and John have actually been getting along much better," America said as she continued to defuse the situation.

"I don't know how you can forgive him after he tried to tank Christmas Cove last year." Following America's directions, Poppy moved ahead as well. "What if I have to stop?"

"Aim your toes inward toward each other." America demonstrated. "I really don't think he's a bad guy. I just think they misjudged one another and made poor choices with their behavior. We all do that sometimes."

Poppy came to a stop like America explained to her and raised her right brow. "You're saying I should take him off my hit list?" Poppy grinned and took off across the rink. "And what about turning?" she yelled from the far side of the ice.

"All you need to do is lean the way you want to go and turn your toes slightly in that same direction," America cupped her hands around her mouth and yelled back. "Try it."

While trying it, she turned right into John's arms. Even from where America balanced across the rink, a visible blush warmed Poppy's cheeks and John looked like he had never held a beautiful woman in his arms before. In the light from the van's headlamps and the bonfire, his face looked ghostly. He bumbled through asking her if she was alright. Poppy shoved him, though he didn't budge, and as a result, pushed herself backwards into the snowbank.

He stood over her, hands on his hips, and laughed. "Do you want my help now?"

"Haven't you done enough around here?" she said. "I will never want you to do anything for me, Mister Mayor Thorpe." As if her words weren't message enough, she threw a snowball at his chest, and it broke into a cloud of tiny crystals.

"What do you think about that?" Leo said as he came up behind America.

"I didn't know you were there." She leaned into him for a kiss, and he dodged her advance nearly causing her to pitch forward over her toe pick.

"Enemies, remember."

"I recall," America said with disappointment dripping off her pouting lips. "As for John? He angered the wrong woman last year. It's a surprise she hasn't socked him sooner." America chuckled as the two rivals carried on their snowball fight at the other end like they were the only ones there.

"I'm exhausted," Leo said and pulled America to where the drinks were cooling in the snow. Taking the spout, he poured

Pa's beer into two disposable red cups. "Try it. Pa said it's one of his best."

"You know I don't like beer," America said and sniffed the liquid.

"You'll like this one."

America brought the rim of the cup up to her mouth and tilted the cup just enough to let the beer hit her lips. It tasted nothing like the other beers she had tried, but Pa had a way of never giving up on a lost cause. In this case the lost cause was getting America to like a beer. Tomorrow, she hoped Pa wouldn't give up on his other lost cause, Carol.

"It tastes like apples. Or is that..." she swished some around her tongue, "Figs?"

"So, do you like it?" Leo said with smiling eyes in hopes that this new flavor might be the one to crack the code.

"It's the best one I've tried," she said generously, but his face deflated. "I'm sorry. I just don't like the way beer tastes like swamp water, even if it is fig-flavored swamp water."

"And how much swamp water have you tried?" Leo said with a tone smacking of incredulity.

America skated away. "I'll never tell." She realized her response left the door open for him to assume she had tried a lot of swamp water over the years, which came with a certain ick-factor, but this was war, and she had already entertained the man long enough.

On one side of the rink, Carol and America's mom had patted down and created a makeshift bench area where the women amassed like soldiers ready for battle. America placed her cup in the snow and sat to retighten her laces. "That's Pa's beer if any of you want to try it."

Carol reached across in front of America and took the red cup. "I'll take it. After all, I might need to get used to being his permanent taste-tester," she said under her breath where only America could hear.

Or so she likely thought.

"Why?" Thandie asked and appeared from behind Carol's shoulder. "Why are you going to his permanent taste tester?"

"I don't know what I'm saying. Silly old brain," Carol said and sipped the beer.

"Is there something going on between the two of you?" Thandie egged her on.

"Something," Carol said while America played dumb, adding only a shrug.

Jenny skated towards the group and did a pretty spin with her arms over her head like a ballerina and her foot cocked out to one side. She spun faster and faster, eventually coming to a stop and doubling over with her hands resting on her knees. "I haven't done that in years."

"If this was a figure skating competition and not a hockey game, I'd say we would win," Vivian said and put her arm around Jenny. "But we had better get this game going. Someone's going to have to clean out Bingo's stall in the morning, and it's not going to be me."

"Come on girls," Thandie said. "Huddle up." They gathered in a circle. "I have a plan. It's a bad one, but it might just work."

"I don't want to clean Bingo's stall, either. Whatever your plan is, I'm in," Carol said, and the others nodded along.

"As far as I see it, we're evenly matched, and I don't mean by our hockey skills. But look, I have Grant, Jenny has Cam, America has Leo, Vivian, you have Paul. Carol? You can take on Pa. And Poppy, do you think you can take John out?"

"It would be my pleasure," Poppy said with a smirk and squinted eyes that should have terrified any man. "What do you have in mind?"

"Well, this might sound controversial, but bear with me." Thandie leaned in and giggled her words. "I say we use what the good lord gave us and distract them as much as possible from their goal. Then, if you see an opening, any shot, you take it."

"Oh, I got this," Jenny said. "Cam can't take his eyes off me lately. This will be a breeze. Just a little hair flip, and smoldering eyes and he won't know which way he's heading."

"To the bedroom, probably," Carol joked.

"Carol!" America scolded.

"What?" She looked as innocent as a jackal. "I know things."

"So, we all know what to do?" Thandie said and put her hand in the center of the space between them. "On three, ladies?"

"One."

"Two."

"Three."

CHAPTER 26

"Do you hear all that feminine energy over there, men?" Leo said and gathered his friends into a huddle. "I think these women mean to win tonight. And are we gonna let them?"

"NO!" they shouted back and patted each other on the backs like winners.

Leo waited for their attention to fall back on him. "Alright, who's played hockey before?" Grant raised his hand, and Cam waved his palm up and down like he was unsure. "I vote Grant as team captain."

"I should be upfront and tell you I haven't played since I was eight years old," Grant said.

"And I haven't played any since college, and I only played with some friends in a frozen over parking lot," Cam said.

"Okay, so we probably can't win on merit, but…" Grant shook his head. "What if we just use what we've got and make the girls forget about the game so much that we can sneak a shot in every now and again. Simple. Distract, score, and win. We get the pot of money. They get to clean up horse sh—"

"Grant Goldie, I don't believe my ears," Pa scolded him with a single look. "You want us to win under dishonest circumstances?"

"Yes," Grant said with no hesitation. "Are you all in?"

"I'll take America," Leo said.

"I bet you will," Cam joked. "I obviously have Jenny, and none of you better come near her." He pointed a finger towards each of the other guys while making eye contact.

"I'll take Carol," Pa said and slapped Paul on the back. "You got Vi."

"That leaves you, John," Grant said. "You get the city girl."

"You sure I can't take on Thandie?" John pleaded with his hands in prayer. "Poppy already has it out for me tonight."

"Thandie's all mine," Grant said, and his brows raised in three pulses.

"To be young again," Paul lamented. "Who's gonna faceoff?"

"Leo and America, of course," Cam said. "Now, let's out-do their sorry attempt at intimidating us and shout like the highlanders we are."

"But we're not," John laughed nervously.

"That's not the point, brother. Let's give it what we've got," Leo said and counted to three.

The men let out a battle cry with whoops and shouts that Braveheart would be proud of while they skated to the unmarked center. The women turned and skated arm-and-arm to meet them like a formidable roman phalanx. The men lined up in front of the girls and waited for the ref to appear.

Beside the fire, Alfonso was bent over, though Leo was unable to see what the man was doing. "Alfonso. We're ready to get started."

Instead of an answer, music carried through the night air. A strong downbeat, drums and guitar picking that perfectly matched the atmosphere. Leo knew the song before the verse even started. 'Long Cool Woman' by The Hollies was one of his favorites, and a great tune to get this game on.

Alfonso ran straight to the center, bypassing the cleared snow, and barreled over the heaps that made up the boundary lines.

With the glowing puck held high over his head, he used his finger to draw America and Leo to himself.

The way America smiled and bit her lip, undid him. Leo just wanted to get this game over and get her home. He locked his gaze on his stunning wife. *This is going to be a cake-walk*, he thought and blew her an air kiss.

She moved her head to the left and mimed catching the kiss on her cheek. "You're going down, Leopold," she said, though he was unsure whether her words were a threat or an invitation.

"Ready?" Alfonso said. Leo nodded followed by America. "Faceoff!" he said as the puck fell from his fingers and bounced on the ice. Before the puck came to a rest, Alfonso turned and bolted off the rink.

America was first to get her stick on the puck and shot it over to Jenny to her left. Jenny caught the puck and skated with one leg off the ice and stretching skyward, like a figure skater. She spun and shot the puck across to Carol who took it clear to the small goal. Before Pa could even catch up to her, she swung her stick and took the shot.

Cheering overtook the sound of 'Rocket Man', which was now playing from the speaker.

"One score to the *bella donne*," Alfonso said and held up one finger.

"Are you on their side?" Grant asked.

"Alfonso not take sides." He motioned for Grant to come to the center, and Thandie came in too.

Leo stood beside Grant and was determined to not underestimate the women again. America paired with him with one foot in front of the other like a runner ready to take off. But she wouldn't get past him this time. She looked over to Carol and they nodded like they were sending messages telepathically, which didn't bode well for Leo or Pa, he suspected.

Alfonso dropped the puck, and instead of focusing on the faceoff, Leo focused on America. He skated toward her, using his stick as a guard on one side and his arm hemming her in on the other. She dodged his advance and ducked under his arm. Coming around to his back, he felt a stick move up the inside of his leg and goose him on his rear.

There was no way he was going to let that slide. "Get over here," he said and chased her down, barely missing John and Poppy who were fighting over the puck.

America spun around and bumped John off balance, allowing Poppy to steal the puck and shoot it over to Carol. She swung her stick and went for the goal again. The puck ricocheted off the goal post and slid back toward the center of the ice.

There was no apparent organization on either team. Bodies skated in all directions across the rink. Cam and Jenny were sitting in the snow, making out. Pa moved up the ice but was three short strokes behind Carol, and Poppy and John were pointing fingers at each other's faces. Grant and Thandie looked to be having the best time racing across the ice toward the puck, and America was intense and flirty, like she had been when Leo had first met her. After the insane week they had just had, his heart was glad to see her being herself again.

While Leo was distracted by his wife's exuberance, Grant screamed by Leo and clipped America's shoulder. She spun, losing her balance, and Leo seized the opportunity to catch her. She fell in his arms just as the song changed to 'More Than a Feeling'. He leaned down and kissed her on the mouth. Their lips fit so tightly together. Her arms circled his neck, and she played in the back of his mussed hair the way he liked. This is how their night had begun before being kidnapped and he knew the only way to get back to what he wanted was to finish the dang game.

Knowing what had to be done, Leo dropped America down to the ice and skated away from her before she knew what hit her. "Sucker!" he yelled into the cold air.

"This is war now!" America shouted from behind him.

At the women's goal line, Leo circled and waited for Paul who was skating backwards towards him. Vivian was trailing Paul and desperately trying to use her stick to steal the puck from her husband, giggling the whole time. "Pass it back to me," Leo said. "I'm right behind you."

Paul slid the puck between his own legs and away from Vivian. "Not so fast," America said as she intercepted the puck and shot it all the way to the far side and to a waiting Carol. Carol took the puck and shot it right into the goal.

The women circled around Carol and jumped up and down with their arms over each other's backs. From the sound of their cheering, it was though they had just won the Stanley Cup, not a wild hockey game. And if the inevitable men's loss wasn't approaching fast enough, 'Dream On', cut through the night, and cut through Leo's hopes of winning.

"Huddle up men," Leo shouted and called everyone over. Everyone joined him by the other goal, except Cam who was still making out with his wife in the snow. "Hold on." Leo skated across to the two and yanked Cam away. "No fraternizing with the enemy."

Thandie came over and took Jenny by the arm. "We could use your help."

"I was helping," she giggled. "Helping myself to that delicious man of mine."

"Gross," Leo said and dragged a love-drunk Cam to the huddle. "I don't understand what's happening. You need to pull it together and do a better job of distracting them."

Cam's hand flew up. "I was doing just fine, thank you."

"What about you, Pa?" Grant said. "You're supposed to be on Carol and she's killing us right now."

He shrugged. "I didn't know she could play. I swear it. But I'll give it another try."

"And John, whatever is going on between you and Poppy, figure it out."

"She hates me," John said. "She blames me for the

181

incorporation and seems to be personally offended by my presence here."

"Figure it out," Leo said. "I am not cleaning out those stables."

"Yes, you are," Vivian said as she skated a circle around them, stopping behind Paul. Her arms snaked around his torso, and she whispered something into his ear. Whatever she said had Paul slack-jawed and pulling at his collar. She smirked as she skated away.

"You alright there?" Cam said. "I know that look."

"Guys. The women are clearly playing a game with us, and it's not hockey," Leo said having caught on to what they were doing. All the flirting and suggestive banter was their way of distracting the men, and he had to admit, the women were playing the game better than the men were.

"Listen to that," Leo said as 'We Will Rock You', came on the stereo. "Let's finish this!"

On center ice, Alfonso waited, waving the puck above his head.

Pa positioned himself for the face off and pointed at Carol to meet him in the middle. "I want you, here." He pointed to the ice in front of himself.

Answering his request, she skated to his position. "Right here?" she said and pointed to the ice a few feet away.

"No. Here." Pa signaled to the space directly below his nose where he was leaning over.

She swizzled her toes and came so close, she bumped into his shoulder. "Right here?"

Pa was forced to stand up straight to accommodate her proximity. "That's pretty good," he said. Their noses were only a couple centimeters apart.

America looked at them and then at Leo with a smirk. Vivian covered her smile with a gloved hand and Leo nodded to Alfonso to drop the puck.

The glowing green disk hit the ice between them. Instead of

going for the puck, Carol's lips touched Pa's and his hands became limp. He dropped his stick, and it bounced off the ice. By the time Leo saw Carol's stick move toward the puck, it was too late for him to get his own stick between them.

Carol shot the puck to a waiting Jenny who took it, while spinning, down the ice. Passing to Vivian, who passed to America, while Poppy and Thandie blocked for them, Carol left a shocked Pa standing at the center. America passed to Carol who swung and pegged the puck right into the back of the net.

That was it. The men were officially on horse doodie duty. And the women would never let them live their loss down. Ever!

The women deserved all the cheering, and Alfonso joined them in their celebration huddle. There was nothing the men could do but clap their sticks against the ice in applause. With heads hanging low, they reluctantly congratulated the ladies on their rather unexpected win.

As though the music selection hadn't been fitting enough, 'We Are The Champions', boomed over the ice and inflated the ladies' egos even more. He could practically see their heads blowing up.

"Good game!" Leo said to America and hugged her. "Are you ready to go home?"

"Am I!?" she said.

They thanked everyone for an unforgettable party and America sat beside the keg where she had left her untied winter boots. Leo took one more cup and filled it with Pa's beer. "I need a good night's sleep after this."

"You're not going home with her," Grant said. It's bad luck to see the bride before the wedding. "Nope, you're staying here tonight. But first…" he skated away and returned with the can of money and the others in tow. "We all agreed that you two should have this. As a wedding gift."

Amidst all the fun, Leo had forgotten that they hadn't told everyone about accidentally getting married in Vegas. Even though he knew all of these people would learn the truth in just a few hours, there was still a pang of guilt squeezing his conscience. He nodded. "I don't know what to say."

"Thank you all," America stepped in and spoke.

"And I guess I'm staying with the guys tonight. Will you be alright?" he asked America.

"We'll make sure she's settled," Vivian said and took America under her arm. "Get some sleep."

If there was one thing Leo knew he could do following the most exhausting week of his life, it was get some sleep. He thanked Vivian and kissed America. "See you tomorrow."

CHAPTER 27

Of all the finished rooms in her half-renovated house, America's upstairs office was the most ideal for having her morning coffee. She sipped the steaming Columbian brew and pulled open the sheer white curtains, hooking each panel behind a gold, palm-frond holdback on each side of the window. Outside, the snow on the ground amplified the mid-morning sunlight and contrasted with the clear blue sky above. The trees and bushes, still bare from winter, wore a layer of frost, and bridged the space between the white of the ground and the azure sky on the distant horizon.

America took another sip and placed her snowman shaped mug on a small beverage table beside a rattan egg chair. She walked across her office and stood in front of her new wedding-day dress. Her mother must have placed it on the dress form after arriving home yesterday. It seemed none of them were taking any chances with the new gown, not that it would show dirt as easily. Her poor white gown, on the other hand, would need some heavy cleaning even if she just wanted to save it or donate it to someone.

Her fingers walked across the crimson lace bodice and down

to the matching silk taffeta skirt. The fabric wasn't cold like she thought it would be, rather it was soft and smooth, more like velvet. Taking the bottom hem in hand, she stretched it wide and flung it out. The layers of tulle and silk ballooned with air and drifted back towards the ground. The end effect was a satisfying bell shape that even Cinderella could appreciate.

Downstairs, the back door in the kitchen opened and closed. "I'll get a cup of coffee and be right up," her mom yelled. Sounds traveled easily through the walls, some of which were nothing more than exposed wooden studs and plumbing. Even so, nothing her mother did was quiet. A mug clinked against the counter and a metal spoon screeched against the side of the ceramic surface, like nails on a chalkboard, as she stirred in her sugar.

"I'm in the office," America said, and Vivian joined her a moment later. "Did you sleep well?"

"I crashed, but wasn't last night the best?" Vivan said with a mischievous grin.

"How long did you know about the bachelorette party? If we can really call it that." America picked up her mug and clinked it with her mom's.

"Honestly, Thandie and Grant had this planned for a while. I called them yesterday and said it wasn't a good idea after the week you and Leo had, but they insisted." Mom paused to drink and sat back in the egg-chair. "You did enjoy yourself though."

"I'm just glad we won the game." America laughed. "I don't think the men knew what hit them."

"Carol hit them. Did you know she could play?"

"Not at all. She said we never asked. As if that's a normal thing to talk about casually. I guess it never came up." America pulled out the desk chair and swiveled it around to face her mom. "I bet Dad was not thrilled about having to clean out Bingo's stall this morning."

"Are you kidding. He's so bored since he retired, he was up

before sunrise and digging around for just the right cargo pants to wear." Vivian laughed. "You should have seen him. He was as giddy as a girl on a first date."

"What do you expect from a retired lawyer? I've been telling him he needs something productive to do, and if he was handy with literally any tool, I would put him to work on getting this house reno moving along a little faster, but you know he can't even use a hammer," America said. A squirrel climbed up the tree trunk outside the window and caught her eye. The critter flicked his fluffy tail, and America opened a little jar of nuts that sat on her desk. She jiggled the window sash and cracked the window open only a couple of inches. It wasn't much, but it was enough to slide a few morsels out onto the sill. "Add this window to the list of things that need fixing." She shoved it closed and shook her head.

"Now that the wedding is wrapping up, maybe it's time we call in some help and finally finish up this project."

"I appreciate it, but you know I want to do this reno on my own."

"I know you do, but consider how much stress and time this," Vivian waved her hands around the room, "project is taking from you. It's not a defeat to bring in some help."

America hated being wrong, but this was one thing she could admit hadn't gone as smoothly as planned. "The work itself isn't so hard, but this house is a historical property which means there is about a million extra steps to getting any of it done. I can't just start knocking walls down and moving electrical when and where I like."

"That's my point. I think bringing someone in who can help navigate all the historical ins and outs, and has an eye for design, would be wonderful. I'll look into it, is that okay?"

America nodded but couldn't divert her gaze from the red dress, her wedding-day dress.

"And consider it a late wedding gift."

"Late? But the wedding is later."

Her mom giggled.

"Oh. Right," America said and slapped her palm to her forehead. "We got married last week. I didn't forget exactly, but this is still the day I've been planning and looking forward to for months."

"And all of your favorite people will be here to celebrate with you."

"Do you think they're gonna be mad when they find out the truth?" Guilt still plagued America at the thought of having lied to everyone whom she cared about.

"Are you kidding me? Today is going to be a day that none of them will ever forget," Vivian said and winked. She stood and craned her neck to see down the street to Carol's house. "Do you think she's ready? Carol?"

"I think she's as ready as she'll ever be. Did you see her kiss Pa during the last period of the game? On the lips?" America covered her gaping mouth with the back of her hand and giggled. "I don't think he ever thought that would happen. He just stood there like a statue while she scored on the guys again. That one moment might have been the best thing I've ever seen. It's up there anyway."

"I think everyone had such a good time last night," Vivian said and rested her bottom on the edge of the desk. "Maybe we could make the hockey game a tradition."

America replayed some of the moments in her mind. Drinking snow-chilled beer, sharing a bottle of sparkling wine with all the girls, mostly Jenny and Carol, and seeing her best friend tell off Leo's brother, all added up to an epic evening. She was unsure whether they could capture that same energy again, but it would be worth a try. "I think that's a great idea." America shot from her seat. "Poppy! She should be here by now. Did you see her this morning? I don't remember seeing her after the hockey game. I was unconscious as soon as my head hit the pillow."

"I know some of them planned on staying out longer. But last I saw; she and John were walking down the shore together." Vivian shrugged and smiled upside down. "Should we call her?"

America nodded and took her phone from the drink table. As she opened her contacts list, the front door creaked, and someone stumbled in. "Poppy," America said in unison with her mom. "Up here!"

Poppy's boots made a thud as she threw them off in the foyer below, and her bare feet labored up the steps. A very hungover redhead stumbled into the office. "Morning ladies," she said with a half-cocked grin. She pushed her disheveled fiery ringlets out of her face and reached for Vivian's coffee. Stealing the mug, she gulped down whatever remained of the lukewarm elixir. "Great party last night."

America and her mom covered their giggles the same way with the back of their hands. "I guess so," America said. "What happened after I left?"

"I'll go get some more coffee. Black," Vivian said and took the empty mugs with her.

"Nothing happened, per se." Poppy flopped into the egg chair that was seeing more action this morning than usual.

"Is *per se* code for Leo's brother?"

Poppy's hand covered her chest, and she huffed an insulted grunt. "I don't take your meaning."

"Yes, you do. And as the bride, I'm demanding you tell me the truth." America put up her right hand over her heart, and Poppy mimicked. "Repeat after me: I, Poppy."

"I, Poppy, swear to tell the truth the whole truth..."

"And nothing but the—"

"Truth. Are you satisfied?" Poppy said and rested her head on the inner egg capsule. Her eyes closed and America clapped her hands together.

"I don't care how hungover you are. You will spill the tea right now." America feigned a serious tone.

"Fine. I told John that what he did to Leo and this town last year was despicable. Of course, he denied any wrongdoing. He explained that it wasn't his fault. It's not like he had it out for Leo, quite the opposite actually. And did you know that he fast-tracked all the permits Leo needed to get The Foundry up and running last year?"

America shook her head, though it made sense. The process had been remarkably smooth.

"He also used the city's tourism funds to waive all the fees that Leo would have been responsible for. Technically, he didn't waive them. He submitted the proposal to the council so it wouldn't look like he was playing favorites, and they approved it. And then, do you remember... coffee."

"Coffee?" America said as Vivian turned the corner into the room with two steaming cups. Poppy had smelled it coming before America had.

Poppy took one of the mugs and blew the steam away from the rim. With her eyes closed, she took a few sips. All the while America combed through things that she should be remembering. With the coffee kicking in, Poppy carried on. "Last year, when you came here to write your first story about the amazing Christmas Cove and thought Leo had been the one to request the feature, only to discover it had been John the whole time?"

"Of course I remember. Isn't that why you were mad at him in the first place?"

"I dislike dishonesty."

Guilt twisted America's gut. "You do?"

"Unless there's a good reason," she smirked and sipped.

The twisting loosened ever so slightly. "And there was a good reason for John's deception?"

"Yes."

Vivian leaned against a bookshelf and prodded, "Well, are you gonna tell us?"

"After Elizabethtown incorporated Christmas Cove, he designated the whole area as a preservation site so that big hotels wouldn't want to build here anymore. And they didn't. The resort shredded all their preliminary permits and left town." Poppy downed the rest of her coffee and smiled at them.

"Then what?" America said.

"John might not have been able to save Christmas Cove then, but he has been saving it ever since." Poppy's smile turned dreamy, and lights danced in her eyes as she gazed into nothingness. "He's always been looking over Leo. Like a guardian angel or something."

Could Poppy's story of the events be true? Leo's older brother, who America had only been around on a couple of occasions, wasn't the bad guy she or Leo had thought him to be? Thinking back over the previous year, America couldn't think of an instance that would prove Poppy's claims to be false. But how could they all have missed the altruism?

"And why did he tell you all these things?" Vivian said and was clearly just as suspicious as America was.

"Would you believe me if I told you that we had a completely not-drunk, wholesome evening together and definitely weren't partaking in any adult activities other than conversing about his job?"

"No." America laughed so hard that tears wet her cheeks. "Have you seen yourself this morning? I don't believe there was an ounce of anything wholesome happening between you two."

A bright red blush splashed Poppy's cheeks. "He really is the sweetest. I think he was just too proud to show Leo. It couldn't have been easy after their parents passed away. You know? And some guys just bottle all that up."

"And you helped him release it all?"

"Oh, stop it," Vivian said and stood between them. "We all get the picture." She turned to Poppy. "You need to take a shower, and quickly. And you," facing America. "it's about time to get you in this dress."

"Carol should be here any minute to get ready with us," America said and ran her fingers along the dress's neckline again. "Pa was going to pick us up in the carriage, but he can't—"

"I already took care of it. I told him it was too cold and that Thandie's picking us up in Jenny's van," Vivian said and pointed at a half-asleep Poppy. "Shower. Go!"

CHAPTER 28

Déjà vu, America thought as she studied the reflection in the floor length mirror. As the dress was slightly too small right in the middle, she held her waist and pushed the fabric towards her spine. Vivian, standing behind her wearing a pretty, peony-pink column dress, worked at clasping the elastic inner corset. America sucked in and raised her shoulders to give her mom a little more room to work with. She knew it would go on, as it had when she first tried it on in the store, but it was a necessary process. Her mom had missed the Vegas dress fitting, but this moment was all the sweeter for it.

"Can you believe that a week ago, I was trying on my pristine, white wedding gown in a salon in Las Vegas? And now, I'm getting ready to walk down the aisle wearing this stunning ruby-red gown, that honestly, I think I like better than the white one, and it's not even my real wedding."

Having fastened the inner layer, Vivian had no trouble raising the outer zipper. The buttons were a different story. With approximately thirty decorative silk-clad buttons to push through little loops, America knew she would be standing there a little longer. She wiggled her knees to move some blood through her tense body as her mom went to work.

"I'm just sorry I wasn't there to see the look on your face when you found out you accidently got married," Vivian said as she slowly moved up the buttons on America's back. "When does the story come out anyway?"

"I wrote up my draft while we were crossing Kansas and I sent it off somewhere in Missouri when we stopped for gas. It should be in the next issue. March."

"There'll be no hiding the truth then."

America shook her head. "All the couples who wed last week will be named in the article. Janowitz thought it would be a nice touch to list them all. So yeah, I guess Leo and I will be included too."

"Does your boss know?"

"I guess if he's read my copy. But Poppy doesn't know."

"What don't I know?" Poppy said as she came into the office, which was now doubling as a dressing room.

America was tired of lying, but also wasn't ready to tell the whole truth. Even though Poppy had stated earlier in the day that she disliked dishonesty, she had qualified that statement by including an exception. America thought she still had a good reason to not tell the whole story yet. So, she settled on a half-truth. "Pa has something amazing planned for Carol today. And Carol thinks she's surprising Pa with something too."

"Carol is doing what?" Carol's voice carried up the stairwell and across the landing.

"Man, you really can hear anything in this place," Vivian remarked.

America, being fully aware of how drafty her house was, should have known better, though it didn't matter whether Carol overheard or not, it was sort of her show at this point anyway. "I said you have a surprise for Edwin today. I was just telling Poppy."

Carol crowded into the office, a generously sized room, but four grown women and countless yards of fabric made for a tighter than comfortable space. "I heard you all banging around up here and thought I'd better join the party. And yes, I have something special planned for Edwin."

"More special than you planting a surprise kiss on him last night during the game?" Poppy teased.

"No more surprising than you fooling around with the mayor afterward," Carol teased right back.

America giggled at Carol's quick wit. "I'm just glad I got out of there before things got too rowdy."

"Did you enjoy your bachelorette party?" Carol asked.

America nodded and acknowledged Carol in the reflection of the mirror. That's when she saw how beautiful the woman was. "Carol. You look stunning. Turn around and let me see you."

As she turned a circle, she whined, "You saw me in this before."

"I know, but you weren't all dolled up like this. Wow!" America took Carol's hands in hers. "Pa's gonna lose himself when he sees you. Are you ready for this?"

"As I'll ever be." Carol shimmied her shoulders and batted her lashes. Her creamy colored dress and sleek hairstyle looked far more modern than America had ever seen her look, and younger too. But the way Carol held her head high with the posture of a ballerina gave a romantic quality to the whole ensemble.

"Why do I feel like I'm missing something here?" Poppy said.

"You'll get it soon enough," America said, but had a hard time not spilling all the beans.

Outside, someone honked a car horn. Vivian leaned over the desk and looked down at the street below. "Our ride is here."

The women grabbed their things and piled into Jenny's van, though Thandie was the person driving, and arranged all the various tons of fabric inside the space. Poppy's dress was the least formal, and most practical, as it was shorter and had far less details to manage. The pink fit and flare mini dress complemented her peaches and cream skin tone and didn't steal the show away from her fantastic Irish curls. She was stunning and was sure to steal a few looks from any number of men, but most likely from Leo's brother, John. Although, with the way Poppy looked, America wouldn't be surprised to see her friend's dance card full later.

"Is everything set? Alfonso is doing good?" America asked Thandie as she ran all the details through her head like a list needing checked.

"You need to stop worrying. This is your day to enjoy. Everything is as you've asked," Thandie said in a calm voice which did serve to ease America's nerves. Even though the wedding plans had changed, she still wanted to please all the guests and give them a good show.

"Thandie, in case I forget to tell you later, thank you for everything," America placed a hand on Thandie's shoulder, as she was sitting directly behind the driver's seat. "Pulling all of this together, on top of your normal duties, probably hasn't been easy, and you've done it with so much joy."

Thandie's hand covered America's for a moment before returning it to the steering wheel. "See, the thing about helping others, is that it feels better when it's given freely. I'm happy to have been a part of your and Leo's wedding journey because I love you guys so much and you both have done so much for me."

"We all love you, America Greene," Poppy said, and Carol popped open a bottle of prosecco.

Carol took a swig and passed the bottle to Vivian who passed it to America.

"Is this what we're doing now, drinking straight from the bottle like vagabonds?" America said and took a long swig that burned. All the little bubbles popped and sizzled on the way down. She passed the bottle to Poppy, who waved it off.

"I think I've had just about enough to drink in the last twenty-four hours, don't you? Okay, don't answer that," she chuckled in her throat.

Thandie pulled the van to the back of the little chapel that sat tucked away on The Foundry property. Since opening the resort, they had hosted a few weddings on site. During the summer months and into the fall, it had been no issue to have the ceremonies outdoors or in tents, but as it was most definitely winter now, an indoor option had become a necessary next addition. The men had spent the last few weeks building and finishing it out, and just in time, it seemed.

America could still smell the fresh white paint as she followed her mom through a rear door where there was a small vestibule and two sitting rooms. One presumably for each side of the wedding parties to relax in before the ceremony. A narrow hallway wrapped around one side of the chapel and connected the vestibule to the front lobby where she and Carol would enter soon.

As she paced the small room, exchanging looks, and the bottle, with Carol, she was uncertain which of them were more nervous. America and Leo had some explaining to do, but if all went to plan, the guests would be so distracted by what Carol had planned that her and Leo would be off the proverbial hook. She hoped.

Thandie and Vivian had gone inside while America and Carol danced around one another. "Do you know what you're going to say?" Carol asked.

"Shouldn't I be asking you that?" America laughed nervously. "Or are you just planning to blurt out that you love him?"

"I'm going to say something like that, yes."

A knock came at the door and Thandie poked her head inside. "You two ready?"

Carol nodded. Up until now, nothing would seem amiss to anyone who didn't know there was a scheme at play. Carol was America's maid of honor and that's how they intended to carry on for a short time longer. America took her bouquet and shook the water from the stems. "You did a wonderful job with the flowers," America said. The bouquet appeared rustic, as though picked from the wild. The reds, and pinks mixed with soft lavenders and lush greenery. It was a perfect bouquet for a wedding day and complimented her red dress perfectly.

At the door, America nodded to Thandie who revealed another bouquet from behind her back. This one was dripping with tiny white and yellow flowers surrounding several sunflowers. She handed the bouquet to Carol.

"This is for me? But how did you know about the sunflowers?"

"I called Thandie to see if she knew what sort of flowers you had liked at the warehouse."

"It's…" she paused and swallowed her emotions. "Thank you, America." Carol turned and took up the front position. America, in her ginormous dress that swept both baseboards along the hallway's sides, walked behind Carol. In the lobby, Carol waited just to the side of the open arched doors and turned to America and held her hands. A clamor of hushed voices indicated that the little chapel was full of waiting guests, but Carol's gaze was locked on to the flowers in her grasp. "Do you think he'll say yes?"

"After that kiss you planted on him last night, I think he'd be an idiot not to."

"You do know you're talking about two people that needlessly spent more than three decades pretending to loathe one another for the sole purpose of maintaining face, even though all the people who would have ever minded, are long gone?" Carol rolled her eyes at herself. "It sounds so absurd saying it out loud."

"I think what you're doing is beautiful. Now let us get this show moving." America leaned forward and kissed Carol's cheeks. "I'm right here with you."

The music began, a solo violinist positioned at the front of the chapel began the arco to the tune of 'Sweet Child of Mine', Carol's last-minute pick. America held in a giggle as the woman turned the corner and began down the aisle. A smirk plumped Carol's rosy cheeks as she struggled to keep her emotions contained.

From just inside the door, Thandie nodded to America that it was time for her to begin her walk. She took a deep breath, though she wasn't nervous for herself anymore, she just wanted Carol and Pa to be happy. "You look stunning."

Taking the skirt and fluffing it, America spun around and wiggled her hips to settle the underskirt. Her red dress was sure to elicit some gasps from the guests. The song ended and the violinist began playing a score from her favorite movie, Pride and Prejudice. 'Dawn'.

Stepping into the doorway, an audible surprise swelled like a ripple on water as everyone got a glimpse of her unconventional gown. Little did they know just what that poor white dress had gone through over the last week, nor why she was in a red gown. As red was her favorite color, many likely thought the color to be intentional, though unexpected. The thought crossed her mind why she hadn't gone in this direction to begin with. She settled the question on her constant need to meet other's expectations for her.

As she stepped forward and owned the secret that she was carrying, her eyes set upon Leo's. He stood just to the right of center at the end of the lace aisle runner, his jaw relaxed, and he exhaled what looked to be a long-held breath. As he sucked in fresh air, his eyes lit up and he blinked back tears. Even though they were already married, they had been denied a moment like this one. As she approached Leo's position, she mouthed, *I love you.*

I know, he mouthed back, and she about lost all of her composure. Carol quietly cleared her own throat. America knew better than to mess with Carol and righted her face.

CHAPTER 29

Carol stood to the side across from Leo and Edwin, where maids of honor are supposed to stand, and watched America make her way down the aisle. Regardless of America's legal marital status, she made a stunning bride. To everyone in the chapel, America was the picture of elegance and happiness. Her gentle smile showed no hint of nerves or discomfort. Carol's stomach, on the other hand, was a ball of tangled wires slowly electrocuting her to death from the inside out. Or so it felt.

The last time she was this tense was the night she had saved Edwin's life outside the winter formal. That night, she hadn't even been able to cry due to the sickening sensation brought about by the adrenaline that flooded her system. Today was different. She needed to ground herself and look at Edwin for fear of bursting.

Edwin matched her spot about six feet away to her left and just behind Leo's shoulder. Without moving her head, she shifted her eyes from America over to Edwin. His face was alight with joy. Only his eyes weren't trained on America, his were locked on Carol. The terrible knot in her stomach became a thousand butterflies that swarmed into her chest. Focusing back on America instead, her heart pounded against her ribs.

America mouthed *I love you*, to Leo. She caught Carol's gaze for a moment as she approached and gave a small nod. It was now or never, but Carol pleaded with America, with a single look and a clearing of her throat, for a savior from what she was about to do. But America only smiled, having not received the distress signal.

The officiant stepped forward as America and Leo stood face to face. "Dearly beloved, we are gathered here today to witness the union of America Greene and Leopold Thorpe. If there is anyone here who objects, speak now or forever hold your peace."

Even though Carol was hiding behind America at the moment, she heard a slight giggle, and Leo bit his lips between his teeth. His eyes fell on Carol, indicating it was time. "I need to say something. Sorry America and Leo, but..." she said and wanted to crawl in a hole. In all her years, she never imagined breaking a wedding ceremony in this way. It was something that happened in sappy romcom movies, not in real life and certainly not in hers.

America stepped to the side and backwards, effectively switching places with Carol. Leo did the same thing with Edwin and pushed him forward.

"What's the meaning of this?" Pa said and tried shoving Leo back to the center spot.

Leo, knowing what had to be done, thrust Edwin towards Carol. He kept a hand on Edwin's shoulder for good measure.

"You got this," America whispered from behind Carol.

But did she?

"Carol? What's going on?" Edwin said.

"I..." She fiddled with the flowers in her hand and plucked a yellow petal from one of the sunflowers nearest her fingers. "Edwin, there's something I've been meaning to tell you."

"Right now? Here?" His brows were threatening to climb off his forehead.

Carol took a deep breath and waited a moment for it to sink in—that this wedding was no ordinary affair. "Forty-odd years ago, I fell in love with a boy. And forty years ago, I saved that boy from the wrath of a drunken man. My heart broke that night in a way that I allowed to remain in pieces for far too long. I let that shattered version of myself become my whole identity and hurt that boy more in the long run than I ever intended."

Carol turned to America and caught a glimpse of all the guests wiping tears from their cheeks. America nodded once and placed a hand on Carol's lower back.

"I've been a villain in my own story for long enough. A million bandages could never cover the cuts I made, but I'd like to try. Even if takes the rest of my life."

"About that—" Edwind began.

"I'm not finished," Carol interrupted and handed her flowers to America. She took Edwin's warm hands in hers. The rough calluses of his palms were a comfort to her knowing that this boy, this man, would work as hard to keep them close as she had worked at keeping him away. If he would have her. "I... I love you."

Edwin stood there, silent, and Carol swallowed her fear like a lump of dough down her throat. "Say something," she whispered and glanced into the crowd of faces. Dozens of eyes bore into her. She cleared her throat and felt America's reassuring hand on her. *Take a breath*, she told herself.

"Carol," Edwin said with wide glassy eyes. "I have loved you since the moment I met you. Even though you hated me, why do you think that I moved back to Christmas Cove after the war? I had to be near you, even if that meant the only interaction that we ever had was when you were carping about something."

"I never hated you. Not even for a single minute," she admitted. "I only despised myself for the way I treated you. And everyone else." She turned to the guests and said, "Sorry about that, by the way," which drew a few giggles and a *we love you*, from someone near the back.

When Carol turned back, Edwin was down on one knee in front of her, offering himself to her. She covered her slack-jawed mouth with her hand and felt tears pushing at her waterline.

"Carol Noel Smithe, it would be my greatest pleasure to have you as my wife. Will you agree to marry me?" Edwin looked up at her with a broad smile and pinched brows as he awaited her reply.

Leo leaned in and handed Edwin a faded yellow velvet box. Edwin opened the lid and held it up to her. She opened her mouth to speak but no sound came out. For the first time in her life, she had no snarky remark, no complaint, nor any other words in mind but joy.

"Is this what happiness feels like?" She nodded her answer before the words came out. "Yes. I will marry you. Right now. If you want."

Edwin took a silver ring out from a little box and slid it up her ring finger. It was a perfect fit and the yellow stone attached at the center glittered like a sunrise. *Dawn*, she thought, *just like our new beginning*.

He stood and wrapped his arms around her back, lifting her off the floor by an inch or two. He buried his head in the crook of her neck and kissed the spot below her ear. "Carol." His whisper prickled her skin and she leaned into his embrace.

"How did you know?"

Edwin pointed at Leo with his head. "I've been holding on to that thing for a very long time," he said, and she knew he wasn't lying by how old the box looked. "Now kiss me like you mean it," he told her.

"Yes, sir," she said through a grin; anticipation igniting in her heart. Their kiss at the hockey game was only a tease, a prelude to what would come now.

Their lips met and he swung her in a circle. Her heartbeat thumped in her ears over the applause and cheers coming from the guests, and she thought she might fall to pieces right in front of everyone. This time, she wouldn't be a broken woman, she would be shedding the years' worth of walls she had built. She was showing everyone who she really was, and Edwin would be alongside her every step of the way.

Leo stepped between the lovely pair and the guests. He put his hands up. "Alright, alright. I suppose we have some explaining to do."

"You're not getting married today?" Cam said from his place sitting in the front row.

"We are not," America said and joined Leo by his side.

Carol was too giddy to do anything but observe the reactions of the guests.

Leo held America's hand high in the air, as they looked from each other to their loved ones and friends. "We accidentally got married in Vegas last week."

"So," America continued. "We can't get married today because we already are."

The crowd was full of shocked faces and murmurs.

"We're sorry for the ruse, but we still wanted to celebrate our union with each of you."

"And they couldn't let all this go to waste," Edwin said.

Carol's eyes went wide. "You knew they were already married?" she asked Edwin.

His head tilted towards Leo again and he gave a shrug "So, are we going to do this today?"

Carol looked from Edwin to John, "Well, Mister Mayor?"

"I'll allow it. So long as you come to city hall Monday morning."

Carol nodded at Edwin and the officiant proceeded with the vows. She knew her mouth was moving, and sound was coming out, but all she could hear was the beating of her own heart. Her mind began to clear as a wide smile spread across Edwin's face. His eyes glassed over, and his head tilted to one side. A thousand thoughts were exchanged between them through the tiny movements in their expressions. Apologies. Healing. Expectations. Love.

"For as long as you both shall live?" the officiant said. "You may now kiss the bride. Again."

Edwin used his arm to hold the small of her back. He palmed the side of her face and neck, and his thumb brushed along her jawline, causing her lips to part ever so slightly. He dipped her backwards and cradled her with more love than she thought possible. His silky lips grazed against hers with increasing pressure and passion until they were joined together. A small moan escaped her throat at the most delicious contact she had ever experienced. When he was done sealing their union, he helped her stand tall again.

Carol took a much-needed breath and smoothed her bodice and skirts, as everyone stood and clapped. With a smile so big it might actually fall off her face, she and Edwin ran back down the aisle into a bright future.

CHAPTER 30

Having been separated from his bride for far too long, Leo waded through the sea of wedding guests. He glued his eyes to the back of America's head. Her long dark hair hanging in gentle curls to her waist. A waist that begged to be handled. Her crimson dress spilled across the floor like an invitation to come to her.

He was tired of speaking politely to each and every one of their guests, tired of answering questions about the wedding and the road trip, and tired of pretending he wanted to be somewhere he wasn't. Dinner had been wonderful, and he had sat beside America the whole time, but being positioned at the front of the room with all those watchful and questioning eyes boring into him, wasn't his idea of a romantic meal.

Their sweet Valentine's date in Vegas now seemed all the more perfect for how private it had been. Their road trip that had followed had been one of the best times of his life, he knew that now. Nothing could replace that intimate time that he was able to share with his love. But one thing that had been missing from their unexpected wedding and subsequent adventure in the car, was having that first dance with his stunning wife. An oversight that he was committed to remedying.

A violinist plucked a string, then another. The staccato notes beat in time with his heart. Each step, another note, each heartbeat, closer to America.

He placed a hand on her upper back and traced the buttons descending to her waist. She turned with glimmering eyes, happy eyes, and a grin—his favorite one-sided grin—pulled her cheek up. "May I have this dance?" he asked and presented his left hand for her.

Carol and Pa looked on with giddy excitement as a stunned and radiant America took his hand without saying a word. Her fingers glided over his, allowing him to take control of her body. He used his right hand resting on the space where her bodice and skirt came together and spun her to face him. Her breath caught when her chest collided with his and he liked how their bodies fit together.

Heat coursed through his fingers where their palms touched. Another pluck of the violin string and a long pull of the bow wrapped them in anticipation. Releasing her waist, he directed her to the center of the room under the crystal chandelier that spread the candlelight around the room like a million little stars. Another violin joined the first and the music built along with the desire between him and America.

They had danced before, but never like this. Never as husband and wife in a room they built, filled with the people whom they loved, and knowing that this would be the only first dance they would have. With the dance floor cleared, Leo presented America in a large arc around himself. Gasps and cooing could be heard coming from those watching the entertainment, which only spurred Leo to want to give them the best show.

As America came around the full circle, he yanked her and spun her inward into him. His arm wrapped fully around her body and their free hand touched at the fingertips. He kissed her nose and flung her back away from his body. She giggled and bit her bottom lip between her teeth. Oh, how he wanted to free that lip from its temporary trap.

Taking her right hand in his, he stepped in time with the music, leading her in a large pattern around the space. Her dress swooshed along the wooden floor and firelight flickered in her eyes anytime he came around the side of the room by the stone fireplace. Joy oozed from her with every rock and sway of her hips.

Holding her close was nice. He buried his face in her hair and smelled the warm vanilla and floral scent that was activated by their vigor. Feeling her pulse pound against his lips when he kissed the spot on her neck just below her ear, was the best thing he had ever felt.

The music began to quiet, and he dipped her low, taking her entire weight on his forearm. From here, she couldn't go anywhere, and he liked it that way. He bent his neck down and met her face to face. Her labored breathing threatened to break the bindings of her dress. Her chest heaved up and down from the exertion and he took the moment while she caught her breath to take in her silky skin glowing in the low light. He wanted to sear this image into his mind forever.

Her lip quivered and he was desperate to give America what she wanted. His lips crushed against hers, taking her breath away in a new form. He felt the subtle vibration of pleasure shiver through her and only broke their kiss because he was smiling too wide.

"Are you ready to get out of here?" he asked, already knowing the answer.

She nodded and dabbed the corners of her mouth with the back of a finger.

Leo lifted her from the dip while the guests clapped for them. It was a show they had come for, and it was a show in which they had gotten way more than they had anticipated. The entire day had been a beautiful celebration of their love for one another.

Carol and Pa joined them on the dance floor. "Thank you for the most beautiful wedding we could have never planned ourselves," Carol said and took America's hands in hers.

"Because you two would have never gotten out of your own way long enough to see what was right in front of you this whole time," America joked. "You just needed a little push—you both did the rest."

"That we did," Pa said and nudged Carol's shoulder. It was obvious their days of giving each other a hard time weren't over, but Leo supposed this was the way they had been showing their affection to each other for a very long time whether they knew it or not.

"I have one question," America said, her face losing all the joy that had just been present. "Which one of you picked the stew?"

Carol and Pa looked at each other, then back to America, and back at each other—the final time with fingers pointing at the other person. They laughed. "It was you," Carol said.

"I believe it was you," Pa accused back.

"I haven't lost my memory, Edwin. It was only a few days ago that you and I sat right over there, and taste tested all the food. It was you who ate two whole servings. One of which was mine. And don't get me start—"

"Enough!" America and Leo said in unison causing the couple to quit their bickering.

"You two have a lifetime to fight over it. Needless to say, it was unexpected and delicious," Leo said.

Carol nudged Pa. "See, I told you."

"I'm glad this all worked out. Pa, Carol. Congratulations," America said and kissed Carol's cheeks. "We're going to call it an evening."

Thandie and Grant walked hand in hand like they were on a mission and laser-focused on the four of them standing in the center of the room. "You weren't thinking about leaving without going to the Grove, were you?"

"I nearly forgot," Leo said and kicked the invisible dirt in front of his foot. "Let's get it over with," he said.

Outside, Thandie and Grant sat in the front seat of a golf cart and held two shovels and a large cardboard box on their laps. "Get in," Thandie said.

Carol and Pa took the two seats directly behind Thandie and Grant, while Leo was content to have America to himself in the rear facing seats in the back, their legs dangled off the back, his nearly brushing the gravel drive, while America held all of her fluffy skirt layers in a pile in her arms. The guests, who were able, followed them out of the Harbour House doors holding lamps to light the way.

They made their way to a spot near the recently repainted white gazebo. A path had been cleared in the snow, no doubt by Grant, that led from the sidewalk to the Grove. Alighting from the golf cart, Leo helped America walk through the snow, her shoes would likely be ruined, but participating in the new tradition would be worth it.

Grant handed a shovel to Pa, and one to Leo. "You know what to do," Grant said and shined a larger spotlight where they were to get to work digging their holes.

Leo's shovel went right through the loose snow and crashed into the frozen ground hidden beneath, while the flash from the photographer caught him off guard. He had nearly forgotten their every move was being documented until then. As he dug the hole, one small shovelful at a time, the symbolism wasn't lost on him that his marriage would be hard work too. But as he and America took the little sapling from Thandie's cardboard box and planted it in the earth, he knew that all that hard work would pay off.

As beautiful as the occasion was, Leo did most of the work, since America's dress was so gigantic, she was in no position to offer much more than encouragement. Even so, he was glad to shoulder this one, this time. Carol on the other hand was right down in the dirt, kneeling down beside Pa. They patted the ground around the sapling's root ball.

"They really are happy, aren't they?" Leo said.

"As happy as I'll be when I can get out of this dress." America winked and began trudging back up the hill.

"Wait up!" he said and hurried behind her.

They ran, hands linked, through the snow until Leo had had enough with all those layers slowing her down. He swooped America off her feet and carried her the last hundred yards to their waiting car. Placing his bride directly in the front seat of his old red pick-up truck, he smooshed her skirt inside the door and closed it before any could fall back out.

Cam held the driver's side door open and shook Leo's hand. "Congrats, man."

"Thanks for everything," Leo said and sat down, pulling the door shut. He leaned out the window and waved at all their loved ones who had come to see them off. Their bags were packed and sitting in the bed of the truck, with their Italian honeymoon waiting. The car pulled out and the sound of scraping tin cans on the gravel caused them to laugh out loud. The silly gesture summed up their week in a way words couldn't. He looked at America, beaming. Her fingers drummed on the little windowsill as she shifted her gaze from their friends waving farewell outside, to his eyes, locking onto him like an eagle. "You ready?"

"Now. Always," she said, and the layers to her answer had him swallowing the possibilities of her meaning down his throat.

He intended to spend the rest of his life uncovering all the ways she loved him and showing her the depths of his heart. A love he no longer wished to compare to anyone else's. It was theirs alone. A love like no other.

RATE AND REVIEW

We hope you enjoyed *A Winter's Wedding* by Sarah Dressler. If you did, we would ask that you please rate and review this title. Every review helps our authors.

Rate and Review: A Winter's Wedding - Book 3

MEET THE AUTHOR

Originally from Florida, Sarah Dressler's life journey has taken her around the globe. Inspired by her father's military service and later as a military spouse, she pens novels that aim to reach a deeper understanding of the world. With her appreciation for diverse cultures, Sarah's stories touch on themes of family, personal growth, and new beginnings in an uplifting and heartwarming manner.

OTHER TITLES FROM

5 PRINCE PUBLISHING

Visit www.5princebooks.com
Keeping Kama *Emi Hilton*
Soul Sacrifice *Courtney Davis*
Picking Pismo *Emi Hilton*
Spring Showers *Sarah Dressler*
Secret Admirer Pact *Bernadette Marie*
The Pack *E.C. Saulness*
The Taste of Treachery *Emily Bybee*
The Publicity Stunt *Bernadette Marie*
A Trace of Romance *Ann Swann*
Descendants of Atlantis *Courtney Davis*
Holiday Rebound *Emily Bybee*
Rewriting Christmas *S.E. Reichert & Kerrie Flanagan*
Butterfly Kisses *Courtney Davis*
Leaving Cloverton *Emi Hilton*
Beach Rose Path *Barbara Matteson*
Aristotle's Wolves *Courtney Davis*
Christmas Cove *Sarah Dressler*
A Twist of Hate *T.E. Lorenzo*
Composing Laney *S.E. Reichert*